The Hotel Monte Sano

A Novel

by Charles Farley

The Ardent Writer Press, LLC
Brownsboro, Alabama

ISBN   978-1-938667-28-2 (paperback)
            978-1-938667-31-2 (hardback)
            978-1-938667-35-0 (mobi/ebook)

Library of Congress Control Number: 2014946993
Library of Congress subject headings:
- FICTION / Historical.
- FICTION / Coming of Age.
- FICTION / Suspense.
- FICTION / Mystery & Detective / Historical.
- Fiction--romance.
- Nineteenth century--Fiction.
- Crime--Alabama--Fiction.
- Huntsville (Ala.)--Fiction.
- Huntsville (Ala.) History 19th century.
- Huntsville (Ala.) Viduta.

Illustrated

First Edition

Also by Charles Farley

Soul of the Man: Bobby "Blue" Bland
Secrets of San Blas
Secrets of St. Vincent
Secrets of St. Joe

Charles lives in Huntsville, Alabama, a few
blocks from the site of the Hotel Monte Sano.

AUTHOR'S NOTE

THIS STORY IS FICTION. And while the places and some people are real, the main characters — particularly Jude, Sophie, and Smokey — and their actions are not. The author has attempted, however, to make the setting as historically accurate as possible. To that end, he has been assisted in his research by Jane Barr of the Monte Sano Historical Association, B. Susanna Leberman of the Huntsville--Madison County Public Library, Stephanie Timberlake of Burritt on the Mountain, Kent Wilborn and Brian Moore of the Monte Sano State Park, and Brenda Hall, Elizabeth Shriver-Thornton, Soos Weber, and Greg Wright of the Monte Sano Civic Association. In addition, these books have been especially helpful:

- Brands, H. W., *The Reckless Decade: America in the 1890s*, Chicago, University of Chicago Press, 1995.
- Chapman, Elizabeth Humes, *Changing Huntsville, 1890-1899*, Birmingham, AL, Privately Published, 1972.
- Gilbreath, Doris Benefield, *Lily Flagg*, Huntsville, AL, Gilbreath Publications, 2001.
- Litwack, Leon F., *Trouble in Mind: Black Southerners in the Age of Jim Crow*, New York, Vintage Books, 1999.
- Reeves, Jacquelyn Proctor, *Hidden History of North Alabama*, Charleston, SC, History Press, 2010.
- Sulzby, Jr., James F., *Historic Alabama Hotels and Resorts*, Tuscaloosa, AL, University of Alabama Press, 1960.
- Varnedoe, Jr., William W., and Lundquist, Charles A., *Tales of Huntsville Caves*, Huntsville, AL, Huntsville Grotto of the National Speleological Society, 2005.

Photographs and Maps

Period photographs and maps of Huntsville and Monte Sano courtesy of the Huntsville--Madison County Public Library

Nature photographs of Monte Sano courtesy of John Hornsby, Monte Sano State Park

Monte Sano Plateau map courtesy of Littlejohn Engineering Associates

The Hotel Monte Sano map courtesy of David Nuttall, Artimaps, LLC

Monte Sano Mountain map at the end of the book courtesy of Soos Weber and Steve Perkins, Geographic Information Systems, City of Huntsville, Alabama

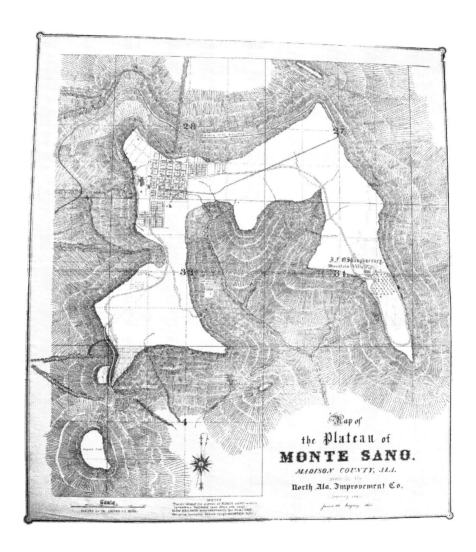

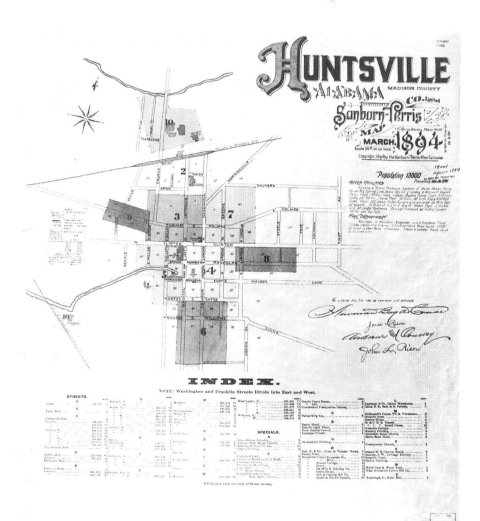

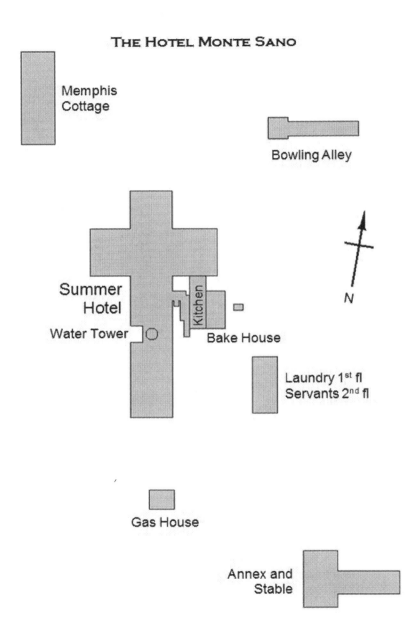

THE HOTEL MONTE SANO

Memphis Cottage

Bowling Alley

Summer Hotel

Kitchen

Water Tower

Bake House

Laundry 1st fl
Servants 2nd fl

N

Gas House

Annex and Stable

They danced and they drove and they rode, they dined and wined and dressed and flirted and yachted and polo'd and Casino'd, responding to the subtlest inventions of their age; on the old lawns and verandahs I saw them gather, on the old shining sands I saw them gallop, past the low headlands I saw their white sails verily flash, and through the dusky old shrubberies came the light and sound of their feasts.

Henry James

Monte Sano crowned with flowers
Guards fair Huntsville's graceful towers
Which like some fair picture bright
Framed in wreaths of purple light
Nestles in the Cumberland grand
In the Sunny Southern Land.

Carolee Pleasants

CHAPTER ONE

THE EARTH SHOOK. *Junior felt their arrival before he heard or saw it — the heavy hooves pounding the clay like thunder around their little cabin on Whitman Creek. And then they were there. He heard the horses snort and scrape, smelled the oil from their smoking torches, and, through a crack between the logs, sighted the fury in their eyes.*

Eight horsemen surrounded the cabin with rifles raised and ordered them out. Caught off guard, Ma and Pa did as they were told. They gathered the children — all nine of them — and herded the family into the dark yard. One of the angry men dismounted and dragged Pa and John, the oldest son, over to the old hickory tree next to the front gate.

"Willis Brooks and John Brooks are hereby ordered to join the Confederate States Army," one of the horsemen shouted.

"Who says?" Pa demanded.

"We do, that's who. The Lawrence County Alabama Home Guard."

"Well, you ain't done nothin' to guard my home, fer as I can see."

"Don't matter. Git to the barn and saddle your horses. You're comin' with us."

"Ain't gonna happen. We already done told y'all," Pa yelled. "We ain't goin'. We don't own no slaves, and we don't care nothin' about fightin' no war. We gotta stay here and take care of these young'uns. Cain't you understand that?"

"String him up!" a horseman ordered.

Two more men dismounted and produced a rough hemp rope with a noose already tied at one end. They placed it around Pa's neck, and one of the men tossed the other end over a low-hanging limb of the hickory tree and pulled it taut. They roughly tied Pa's hands behind his back. Another man dismounted and pulled a leather coil from his saddlebag.

"Mister Brooks, is that your final decision?" he asked.

"Yes, sir, it is."

The man raised his hand and unfurled the whip and then snapped it down quickly, its swift tip crossing Pa's chest with a pop. As the blood stained Pa's nightshirt, Ma screamed and John rushed toward the man with the whip, but he was restrained by the hangman.

Again and again, the man lashed the whip across Pa's helpless body until his shirt was in shreds and he was covered with blood.

"Now, what do you say, Mister Brooks?" the man finally paused and asked.

Pa did not answer, his slashed head slouched to his chest. Then the rope went taut again, as the noose tightened and Pa's body was raised from the ground.

"No!" Ma screamed, as she ran toward him. But the man with the whip stopped her and threw her to the dirt.

John tore to the hangman, but, before he could reach him, a shot rang out and he buckled, bleeding, to the dusty ground. Another shot echoed through the clearing and Pa's body went limp.

And then they were gone, just as suddenly as they had appeared. And John lay dead, face down in the dust, as Pa swung grotesquely in the evening breeze.

Ma untied the rope from the trunk of the tree, and Pa's body fell to the earth with a sickening thud just a few feet from where John lay still. Ma knelt beside John and hugged him and cried. Then she fell over Pa and sobbed. The children followed her.

"Here," she bawled, "wash your hands in yo' poor Pa's blood and vow to me, every last one of you, that you'll find those bastards and kill 'em all."

And the children did what Ma had ordered, huddled there around her and Pa and their big brother John in the bloody red Alabama clay.

"We will," Junior cried. "We'll kill 'em all, Ma. Don't you worry."

The Hotel Monte Sano

CHAPTER TWO

DEAR DIARY,

MAMA TOLD ME at supper tonight that we're going somewhere in Alabama for the summer. Well, her and me and my little brother Jeremy, that is. Papa is going to stay at home here in Schenectady to work on a merger of the company he works for, Edison General Electric, with another company in Massachusetts. I don't know what the big deal is. How hard can it be to put together a couple of companies after all. Anyway, Papa is either at work or worrying about it all the time, so this is really nothing new, as far as I can see.

Papa found out about this fancy hotel in Alabama from this rich man named Vanderbilt who has been financing Papa's company for a while now. Anyway, it's supposed to be real pretty and up in the mountains and real healthy. I didn't know they had mountains in Alabama, but I guess they do, because the hotel is called the Hotel Monte Sano, which Papa says means "mountain of health" in Italian. I didn't know there were Italians in Alabama either, but I guess there are.

Since I had diphtheria this past winter, Mama and Papa want me to go somewhere healthy this summer. I'm feeling fine now, but Mama and Papa are apparently set on this, so we're going to leave next week. Mama says it will take about a week by train to get there. I'm not looking forward to that, especially cooped up with Jeremy that long. Goodness knows, I love him, but he can be so exasperating some times. Mama and Papa baby him something awful. He loves to pick on me, and Mama and Papa never do anything about it. They say that he's only six years old, so I should be patient. Usually I am, patient that is, but sometimes I can't help myself and whack him upside the head. Then, of course, he goes crying to Mama, and I get in trouble.

Besides the long train ride, I don't look forward to being away from my friends all summer. We usually go swimming and horseback riding during the summer, but Mama says I can do that in Alabama too, just without my friends. She says I'll make new friends. We shall see.

So I'll miss Willa and Susan this summer. They both have boyfriends now, so maybe I wouldn't see them that much anyway. I don't have a boyfriend, and I don't really want one, not now anyway. Mama says I have plenty of time. I'm only fifteen after all. Mama says I'm too much of a tomboy to attract boys, but I don't care. I like to play outdoor games and go fishing and ride horses, and if the boys don't like it, that's too bad. I just don't give a damn, as Papa would say.

I have to start packing soon. I have no idea what to wear at a fancy hotel in Alabama, but Mama probably does. Despite missing my friends and having to put up with Jeremy, I'm excited about the adventure of going all the way there, since I've never been to the South before, but I'm a little afraid too, since I don't know a soul down there. Oh well, we shall see, I guess.

Sophie Franklin
June 6, 1892

The Monte Sano Turnpike

The Tally Ho

CHAPTER THREE

JUDE SCHRIMSHER WAS SHOVELING horse manure, as usual, when he heard the arrival bell in the stable ring.

"Tally Ho's here!" his boss A.D. Rogers yelled from the stall that he had turned into a makeshift office in the far corner of the stable. "Git yo' sad ass out there and bring that team around, and saddle 'em up. We got guests waitin' to ride, and we ain't got a single mount left in the barn."

"But they've just come up the mountain," Jude protested. "They need to be cooled and watered and fed."

"Shut up!" Rogers snapped. "Don't argue with me. Git over there now and bring them horses back here."

Jude headed for the hotel. He knew it was not right to hate someone, but he hated A.D. Rogers nonetheless. The hulking man with a bushy, black handlebar mustache that drooped over his constant frown was in charge of the Hotel Monte Sano's stable, but Jude knew more about horses than his boss ever would. But it wasn't just the horses that Rogers mistreated, he abused his employees as well: Jude, the Cherokee Indian Waya, the older, sensible Ivan Demensher, and especially the mysterious, middle-age man named Sherm Williams who hardly uttered a word, unless he was disagreeing with A.D. Rogers, which was happening a lot lately. Rogers, it seemed, was always mad at something or somebody, and no one knew exactly why. But they all knew that he had a real talent for making everyone around him miserable most of the time, like a headache that just wouldn't go away.

The Hotel Monte Sano

The Tally Ho was a large wooden carriage that could haul as many as sixteen passengers and all their baggage from the train station in Huntsville up to the hotel at the top of the mountain called Monte Sano. Jude wasn't sure why they called it a Tally Ho. It was just a carriage, but he had to admit that it was an impressive carriage, with a curved roof, leather-padded benches, and wide windows to view the mountain scenery and panoramic valley views as the carriage wound its way up the Monte Sano Turnpike from the Maple Hill Cemetery and the Union Depot in downtown Huntsville. But Waya, who knew more about horses and animals than anyone, said that someone had told him that the name came from the Crescent Stables and Livery in Eureka Springs, Arkansas, where these large four-in-hand carriages were used for sightseeing and hauling tourists around for holiday parties in the Ozark Mountains.

Even though the Tally Ho was stylish, Jude didn't understand why anyone would want to spend the four and a half, hot and bumpy hours it took for the carriage to ascend the mountain rather than riding the new Monte Sano Railway train that traversed the same distance in little more than thirty minutes. True, the train had experienced an accident soon after the line was completed back in 1889, when the sandbox had jammed and the train had slid down the mountain. Engineer Belue had tied down the whistle to warn anyone on the tracks below and had held steady until the train finally derailed in Fagan Hollow near where the rails crossed the Monte Sano Turnpike. Luckily, no one had been hurt, but everyone in and around Huntsville knew about the incident and many had been leery about riding the line ever since. The only one killed on the railway was a crew member who, in a separate accident, was caught by an overhead wire and dropped to the tracks and run over. So Jude found it odd that people would be afraid to ride the train. He enjoyed it a lot and rode it every chance he got. Sure, it cost a lot of money, fifty cents round-trip, but Jude considered that a bargain.

After the carriage pulled around the circular drive and under the *porte-cochere*, the grand marquee jutting out from the rear entrance of the hotel, Waya and Sherm up front, and Ivan the coachman in the upper rear of the carriage, all in their flashy livery, jumped down and started unloading the baggage. And then a half dozen bellmen, including Jude's daddy, helped the haggard passengers down from the Tally Ho and up the porch steps to the hotel. Jude unhitched the four-horse team from the carriage, grabbed the reins, and started walking them to the stable that was in the annex southeast of the hotel near the road to the coal mines.

"Boss man wants them back in the stable," Jude told Waya and Sherm, "so's some guests can ride them."

"No way," Waya said, his dark eyes flashing. "They need to be cooled and tended to."

"That's what I told him, but he ain't having any of it. Said he wants 'em saddled up and ready to go."

"The man's a fool," Sherm sighed, shaking his head. "I'll be over to talk to him as soon as we get these bags unloaded."

Jude took his sweet time in walking the four big draft horses to the stable. He didn't understand why the guests would want to ride these big beasts anyway. They were bred for pulling and didn't make very compatible riding steeds, as the clopped heavily along. But, of course, most of these Yankee city-slickers didn't know the difference anyway.

Back in the barn, Jude unhitched the sweaty horses from the four-in-hand harness and led them to their stalls. He was bringing a bucket of water to Major's stall, when Rogers walked into the barn.

"What the hell are you doing?" he demanded. "Don't be givin' a hot horse water."

"Why not?" Sherm asked, as he entered the stable with Waya.

"Cause it ain't good for 'em," Rogers blurted. "Everybody knows that."

"Whatta you say, Waya?" Sherm asked. "That right?"

"Old wives tale," Waya said.

A.D. Rogers, his right eye twitching as it always did when he was angry, stood silently in the middle of the stable, spastically blinking at his three dissenting employees.

"Saddle 'em up, NOW!" he ordered, and turned and stalked away.

Carter Chalybeate Spring

CHAPTER FOUR

MR. DENISON TELLS ME he has to go see Colonel O'Shaughnessy, the owner of the hotel, so I can have the rest of the day off. I try to find Jude to go swimming down in Fagan Spring, but he's busy saddling a draft horse for some guest, so I decide to hike all the way down to Periwinkle Spring by myself to check my traps and to cool off down there. A couple of huge boulders have damned up the little stream from the spring to form a fresh, shallow pool, just deep enough to bathe in.

Since Mr. Denison sends me all over the mountain to deliver messages and check on things, I've set out about a dozen or so wooden traps to catch rabbits in. Mr. Denison doesn't allow any hunting or steel traps around the hotel, to protect the guests, but he doesn't mind if I set out a few of these homemade contraptions that I've rigged up. For some reason rabbits don't like to go into wire traps, so I make my traps out of scrapes of pine or cedar boards that I find lying around the sawmill. The traps are just these rectangular wooden boxes, about twenty inches long and nine or so inches high, with a sliding door in front, like a guillotine, that drops closed when a rabbit takes the bait, which is usually a piece of apple or carrot connected to a trigger cord inside and at the back of the box. It's really pretty simple and, to tell the truth, not that effective. First off, I can't remember where I've set the traps half the time. And then when I do find one, more likely than not, the bait's been stolen without the door being triggered. And then if it has been triggered, there ain't nothing in the trap, or there's something besides a rabbit, like an angry skunk, or possum, or snake, or some other such surprise.

If I'm lucky enough to actually catch a rabbit in one of these things, which is maybe about once a month, then I have to kill it, skin it, and gut it. It's a lot of work for what little meat there is to eat on it, but Cook Cazzy in the hotel's kitchen knows how to make it taste really good by baking it in wine and chicken broth, with mushrooms and parsley. And if I'm careful skinning it, I can get a dime for the pelt in Huntsville.

I find a triggered trap just below Carter Chalybeate Spring. I pick it up. Something heavy is inside, might be a raccoon or squirrel. So I set it down and I'm real careful sliding the door open. Then I hear a high-pitched squeal and see the hairs on its tail standing straight up. I jump back and watch as the woodchuck wiggles out of the trap, snarls at me, and then saunters off into the woods. They can be nasty, little critters when they're mad. This one's just a baby or it wouldn't have fit in the trap, but it still has sharp teeth and a mean streak cause it's been stuck in there for who knows how long.

Further on down the steep path into McKay Hollow, I see some movement over in the brush near the little stream that flows over the big, gray limestone rocks when it rains. It looks to be pretty big. I figure it's probably a deer or a fox or maybe even a black bear or panther, so I double back up into the rocks to see if I can get a look at it, whatever it is, before it takes off.

So when I get up there in the rocks as quietly as I can, I look down into the stream bed, and there sitting on a rock with his shoes and socks off and his bare feet dangling in the water is none other than that new gardener they call Will who works for Major Scrimshaw. He's a scrawny, squirrelly sort of fellow, with messy black hair and squinty eyes. And in his skinny hands is a long silver blade almost a foot long with a carved bone handle, and Will is carefully sharpening the blade with a whetstone that he every once and awhile sprinkles with water from the stream. That blade really sparkles in the afternoon sun as I sit watching, unseen by Will, as the knife's edge gets sharper and sharper. After a while, Will dips his left arm in the stream and then takes the knife and starts shaving the hair from his arm. But as he's doing this, suddenly dark red blood wells up from his wrist and streams down to his hand, which he casually places into the stream. And then, as the water turns pink with his blood, Will leans back his head and lets go with a huge laugh that echoes across the hollow like a long whistle on the Monte Santo Railway train. And he just keeps on laughing, like some kind of mad man, while he watches his arm bleed into the water.

And I want you to know, I don't wait around there until he sees me. I back out of there real fast and quiet and run back up the bluff and all the way back to the hotel. By the time I get there, Jude is cooling down a draft horse that a guest has just returned. And, as he splashes the horse with cold water, I breathlessly tell him what I've just seen down in the hollow.

Because me and Jude tell each other everything, even though my skin is as black as a hunk of Monte Sano coal and Jude's as white as a Madison County cotton field in October. Jude and me been buddies ever since two years ago when my boss Mr. Harvey S. Denison took over as manager of the Hotel Monte Sano. It don't seem to matter to Jude what color I am, and I don't care that Jude's a white boy, even if he is a Southern white boy — "crackers," they call 'em down here. We just seem to get along for some reason, maybe cause we're both about the same age and there ain't no other boys around here just coming on to sixteen.

Mr. Denison sort of adopted me, not legally, of course, when I ran away from the Colored Orphan Asylum in New York City three years ago when I was twelve. I never did know my parents. I always lived in the orphanage as far back as I can remember. Me and some other runaways they called Street Arabs was living on the roof of the Grand Central Hotel that Mr. Denison managed down on Broadway. They beat us in the orphanage every time we did something they didn't like, so I just took off one day and took up with these street kids. We scavenged for food in the garbage bins behind the city's big hotels and restaurants and pretty much done as we pleased. And at night we slept anyplace we could find that was warm and out of the way of the police that was always hassling us. At the Grand Central, they had a big steam-heated water tank on the roof, so we slept up there next to it. It was a fairly safe place to bed down too, since, if the police came, we could run and jump off the roof of the building, across the narrow allyway, to the roof of the next building over. No cop was dumb enough to try that, especially in the dark. So the boys in my gang got pretty good at jumping from one building to another, because we all knew what the penalty was if we wasn't good at it. Some of them buildings was ten or fifteen stories high.

Anyway, Mr. Denison found me rummaging through a pile of garbage one winter morning and, for some reason, took me in and gave me a place to stay down in the hotel's boiler room with the colored janitor James, who gave me all kinds of books to read, like *Tom Sawyer* and *Huckleberry Finn*, and *The Life of Ignatius Sancho*, and my favorite, *King Solomon's Mines*. He taught me how to tend the boiler, and shine shoes in the hotel's lobby. I asked Mr. Denison once why he took me in like that, and he just said, "Cause someone was good to me once when I was about your age; now it's my turn." Not to mention that James was getting up there in years and needed help with some of the heavier jobs, like hauling coal and such.

When Mr. Denison got this here job managing the Hotel Monte Sano, he took me along with him, cause James was getting too old to take care of me and was sick a lot of the time, and Mr. Denison needed a gofer to run errands and such for him down here in Alabama. Between errands I help Oliver the shoeshine boy who has a two-chair stand in the lobby right next to Mr. Denison's office.

When the hotel closes in the fall, me and Mr. Denison go into town to take care of the Huntsville Hotel during the winter. Mr. Denison manages the downtown hotel during the summer too, but there's not much business down there then, so we spend most of our time up here on the mountain, where there's lots of guests and all the cool, mountain air you could ever want. When I'm here on Monte Sano, I sleep in the stable instead of in the servant quarters. Mr. Denison told me I could sleep anywhere I wanted, but since Jude and me got to be friends, I've been staying out in the stable. For the most part, I like animals better than people anyway, so it works out okay. Jude's got a little corner over by the carriages where he keeps his stuff and sleeps, even though his daddy stays in his house on the other side of the mountain. Jude says it's a good change of pace to get away from his daddy during the summer and he doesn't have to go so far to get to work every day. I sleep in an empty stall as far away from Jude's boss, Mr. Rogers, as I can get. Ain't nobody that likes that man, including me.

"So, Smokey, what do you think that means," Jude asks me. "That man cutting himself like that?"

"I ain't got a clue."

"Maybe he was just trying to see how sharp his knife was and accidentally cut himself," Jude says.

"But why was he laughing like a crazy man?"

"I don't know," Jude says. "Maybe he *is* a crazy man."

The Nashville, Chattanooga and St. Louis Railway

CHAPTER FIVE

DEAR DIARY,

IT'S BEEN THE LONGEST seven days of my life, and I'm absolutely about ready to shove Jeremy off the side of this mountain now that we've finally arrived on top of it.

First, we took the New York Central and Hudson River Railroad from Schenectady to Rochester, and then on to Buffalo, and finally to Niagara Falls, where we stayed for two days. Jeremy got sick somewhere between home and Utica and threw up all over the place. It was awful. Between the smell, and the heat, and the steam, and the smoke, and the cinders flying from the engine, I almost got sick myself. I know it wasn't Jeremy's fault that he got sick, but it was not a good way to start our trip and not a good way to make friends with our fellow passengers.

It was such a relief to finally stop and get off the train in Niagara Falls. We stayed at the Cataract House Hotel, the biggest hotel in town right on the banks of the Niagara River. We met an old colored waiter there who told us all about his former boss and headwaiter, a man named John Morrison. The waiter said that Mr. Morrison and other free Negro waiters at the hotel ferried runaway slaves across the river to freedom in Canada before the Civil War and the Emancipation Proclamation. Schenectady was also a major stop on the Underground Railroad before and during the War, so we learned all about it in school.

Niagara Falls was really spectacular and much bigger and louder than I had expected. I can't imagine how scary it must have been for Mr. Morrison and those other Negroes to cross this wide, raging river in such small boats. It was scary enough in the larger boat called the *Maid of the Mist* that we took to the bottom of the falls. We all had to wear raincoats to protect us from the spray from the crashing water. Jeremy was fascinated by it all, but buried his face in Mama's raincoat when the boat sailed up to the thundering falls and right into the thick cloud of enveloping mist. At least, he didn't get seasick, but by the time we pulled back into the dock, I was beginning to feel a little woozy myself.

Then we took the train back to Buffalo and changed to the Michigan Southern Railway to Cleveland. The tracks ran right alongside Lake Erie, which looked about as wide as an ocean to me. Jeremy locked himself in the water closet somewhere around Ashtabula and wouldn't come out until Mama threatened to spank him. By then, I was ready to throw him in the lake myself. I'm pretty sure the line of people who were waiting to use the water closet would've gladly helped me out.

We had to change trains again in Cleveland to board the Cleveland, Cincinnati, Chicago, and St. Louis Railway to Cincinnati. Somewhere around Columbus Jeremy decided to run back and forth from one end of the train to the other, until a conductor caught him and brought him back to Mama and me. Mama apologized to the conductor and yelled at Jeremy, who just sat there and pouted for an hour or so. At least, he was quiet and out of trouble for a while.

In Cincinnati, we changed to the Alabama Great Southern Railway which took us all the way to Louisville, Kentucky. When Mama told me a couple of weeks ago that we were going through Louisville, I begged her to let us stop to visit Churchill Downs, a famous horse racing track that they have there. I love horses and horseback riding, so Mama agreed. We went by carriage from the train station to the Scoggan Horse Farm, where they not only raise horses, but also rent rooms. It was real pretty, and they had maybe a hundred or so of these beautiful thoroughbred horses that were as sleek and graceful as ballet dancers as they pranced around the idyllic, green pasture. If Mama would have let me, I would've stayed there forever.

The next day we went to Churchill Downs and I got to see the famous colored jockey Alonzo "Lonnie" Clayton ride a big beautiful chestnut colt named Lookout, one of Scoggan Farm's best young racehorses. Mr. Clayton had become, just the month before, the youngest jockey ever to win the Kentucky Derby, on a horse called Azra, by over two lengths. He was only fifteen and so tiny, just like me. And, at the race that we watched, he rode Lookout to a driving win in a one and a half mile race around the dirt track. It was amazing. Mama let me bet a dollar on Clayton and Lookout, but the bookmakers wouldn't give me very good odds, so I only won twenty cents. But I was happy anyway, even though Jeremy somehow disappeared during the race and we had to search all over the place for him afterward. We finally found him at the restaurant they have there. An old, gray-haired woman in a fancy hat had bought him a strawberry ice cream cone which he was just finishing up when we finally caught up with him. Of course, the ice cream had melted and dripped all over his clean white shirt and he looked a mess. I've never heard Mama curse before, but this time I think I heard her say one of those words that Papa says a lot.

Then it was back on the awful train the next day, this time to Nashville, in Tennessee. Just outside of Louisville, Jeremy snuck away from Mama and me again, and I had to go find him. So I staggered backed through the train as it swayed erratically back and forth and finally found him in the sweltering, smoky club car at the rear of the train, just before the colored car and caboose at the end. There were four men in dark suits sitting around a round table, playing some sort of card game and smoking big old smelly cigars. One of the men, square-jawed and bearded, wore a wide-brimmed Panama hat, and had a lit cigar in one hand and the scruff of Jeremy's neck in the other. Jeremy was crying and moaning and wiggling to get out of the big man's grasp. "Jeremy!" I screamed.

"This one yours?" the man who was holding him asked me.

"Yes, he's my brother. Please let him go."

The man released Jeremy and shoved him toward me.

"Keep him outta here," the man ordered. "We're trying to play cards and can't concentrate with that little brat running around. This car ain't no place for kids anyway."

"Yes, sir," I said, as I collared Jeremy and rushed him out of there, while the men blew gray smoke and laughed out loud at us.

The Hotel Monte Sano

In Nashville, we changed to the Nashville, Chattanooga and St. Louis Railway that took us all the way to Huntsville, Alabama. Jeremy, in short pants, slipped and fell off the stool when we were getting onto the train in Nashville and skinned his knee in the gravel rail bed. I think the conductor who helped him up was sorry he did, because Jeremy just kept on screaming and carrying on like he'd been murdered or something. Mama, of course, babied him, like she always does.

At last, we arrived in Huntsville, only to find out that we had to change to one final train before reaching the Hotel Monte Sano. And guess who sat down across the aisle from us on our way up the mountain? Sure enough, it was the card-playing, cigar-smoking man who had grabbed Jeremy in the club car outside of Louisville. He just frowned at me and then looked out the window, as Jeremy snuggled up to Mama to avoid making eye contact with his former captor. I wanted to tell Mama who he was, but he was right there, so I didn't say anything.

Finally, when the conductor came into our car and introduced himself to us as Dee Yeatman, the big, scary man asked him where the smoking car was. The conductor told him that it was in the last coach on the train, so he got up, glared at Jeremy, tipped his Panama hat to Mama and me, and then headed back to the smoking car. I was sure glad to see him go.

This conductor was a slight, friendly young man, with a syrupy southern accent, who told us all about the train. "This heel dummy-locomotive weighs two tons," he drawled, "and was built by the Baldwin Locomotive Company up north in Patterson, New Jersey. As y'all can see, we've encased it in a body that looks somethin' like a streetcar, and we've built some special noise-reducers to keep the steam and smoke from scarin' the horses and mules as we go through town, down Jefferson Street and onto Clinton, and then up the side of the mountain."

"How far is it?" Jeremy interrupted.

"Seven and half miles," the conductor continued. "Only 'bout thirty minutes and we'll be on top of the world. Well, on the top of North Alabama, anyway."

"Why's it called the dummy?" Jeremy interrupted again.

"Cause it's so quiet. Y'all know, like a deaf and dumb person that can't talk. Like a little gal who come up here with her teacher when the hotel first opened up, back in eighty-eight. Her name was Helen Keller, from over in Ivy Green, and, even though she was blind and deaf and dumb, she wasn't dumb at all. In fact, she was smart as a whip. Why, with a little help from her teacher, she'd carry on a conversation just as good as you and me. I ain't kiddin' y'all.

"Now, let me tell y'all 'bout these heel coaches. All six of 'em was specially designed by a man named Arthur Wilson and built for the Monte Sano Railway Company by the St. Charles Car Company in St. Charles, Missouri. They's only forty-two feet long, as compared to a usual train coach of fifty to sixty feet."

"How come?" Jeremy had to know.

"Well," the conductor laughed, "I was about to tell y'all. But you're fixin' to find out fer your own selves, when we start makin' them short curves as we head up the mountain. Now, that there coach at the end, that one there's got three separate compartments. One with ice in it to keep cold the meat, fruit, and vegetables we're haulin' up from Halsey's to the hotel fer y'all to eat. Another fer yo' bags. And the third fer Negroes and those that wanna take a smoke, like that man I just sent back there.

"Y'all smoke?" the conductor asked Jeremy.

"Uh-uh," Jeremy answered.

The country conductor laughed and pointed out all the local landmarks as the train chugged up the mountain, through thick woods and massive rocks, across high wooden bridges, with many beautiful views of the Tennessee River Valley below. I wrote down the places we rode past: Calhoun Grove and Steel Grove in town, then a place named LaCrosse, Fagan Spring where the train stopped to fill its boiler from a pretty little pool of clear water, O'Brien's Button Hole Bridge where the train travelled over this high, scary wooden trestle, Sylvan Glen, Buena Vista, Cold Spring, Withorn Spring, a little train station at the top of the mountain named Laura's View, and finally, at long last, stopping at the Wise and Company store, and, behind it, the towering Hotel Monte Sano.

The Hotel Monte Sano

I must say that it's much more impressive than I had expected, especially out here in the middle of nowhere. It has two stories and a large sloped attic and has been built right on a high bluff, facing southwest, overlooking the little town of Huntsville nestled in the wide valley below. There's a two-level covered porch that goes almost all the way around the hotel, and a boardwalk along the edge of the cliff, and a double-decked observation tower that looms above it all. Mama says that it was built in the Queen Anne architecture style, which I think means it looks like a big old comfortable country house, or, at least, that's what it looks like to me. It's made of wide wood planks, painted a light cream color, with a high, red, tin roof and even a steeple sticking up into the deep blue southern sky.

As soon as the train pulled in, a whole slew of men descended upon us, dressed in matching uniforms of maroon and gray. While they unloaded our bags, a tall, handsome bellman led us through a gateway of rock-lined flower beds and rows of finely-trimmed shrubbery, up the wide stairs to the hotel's porch and around to the front door on the bluff side of the building. The double doors were decorated with multiple panes of brightly colored glass, and Mr. Denison, the hotel's manager, met us there. He was a neat, well-dressed man in a pressed blue suit and a no-nonsense, business-like air about him. After he introduced himself, the manager immediately launched into a long speech, bragging effusively about the hotel's accommodations.

"Welcome to the Hotel Monte Sano," he began in a familiar northern accent, "the Saratoga of the South. The Franklins, I presume. We've been expecting you."

"Yes," Mama nodded. "This is Jeremy and this is Sophie."

I smiled and tried not to look as tired as I felt. Jeremy just leaned on me and moaned. Mama tried to look attentive and interested, but you could tell that she was just as worn out as Jeremy and I, maybe even more so. But Mr. Denison, tall and thin and wound as tight as a tourniquet, didn't seem to notice at all and continued telling us more than we wanted to know about this grand hotel which he was obviously very proud of.

"Let me first assure you," he declared in his well-rehearsed patter, "that neither money nor pain has been spared in providing you with the most elegantly furnished, first-class accommodations, unequalled anywhere in the South, a true model of convenience and relaxation. It was designed by John Rea and built by L.S. Melbourn in 1887. Here in the lobby you will notice the rich oriental rugs that extend throughout the hotel, as well as the carved wooden paneling, and stained glass windows. The rooms throughout the hotel are heated with steam, although I doubt you'll need it this time of year, and each is lit by gas chandeliers, fueled from three metal cylinders just south of the hotel. And, of course, each room is arranged so that it is naturally lit with a panoramic view of the valley below. There are no back or inside rooms at the Hotel Monte Sano."

Mr. Denison, in his tailored suit and tan spats, then led us through the hotel's lobby that had a big walnut desk behind which rested a callboard and a bank of two-hundred and thirty-three mailboxes and one handsome, smiling, middle-age man outfitted in the same maroon and gray uniform as the men who had met the train.

"The Franklins have arrived," the manager announced. "Mrs. Franklin, Miss Sophie, Master Jeremy, this is Mister Richard Schrimsher, our head bellman and resident expert on everything Monte Sano. He can direct you to the many natural sites and, if you wish to take the waters, to the springs throughout the grounds and tell you which will ease which ailments."

"At your service," the tall, smiling man answered, as he passed a key on a big brass ring to the manager who continued his spiel: "To your left is the Ladies Reception Room and next to it the Main Parlor and Ballroom, measuring forty feet by sixty feet, where you'll find an orchestra for your listening and dancing pleasure most every night. Note the plush bottom chairs and the golden oak Alamo and speaking tables throughout the hotel. And on your right is the stairway and, further down the main hall, our formal dining room. To quote my predecessor, Mr. S. E. Bates, 'the kitchen is the foundation of every good hotel.' Our current *chef de cuisine* is Bubba Conner, the former *sous chef* for the hotel's original chef, the noted Englishman

Jessup Whitehead, who wrote a number of popular cookbooks before his passing in 1889. The chef serves nothing but the finest breads, meats, and vegetables available, as well as Jersey milk and butter from General Moore's Monte Sano Dairy a few miles over on a neighboring mountain. His modern kitchen and fully-stocked storeroom are in a separate building just behind the dining room."

We then followed the manager out onto the porch where he showed us three steel-mesh cages sitting on a wooden table. He read the sign on the cages to us. "Beware of these poisonous snakes. Do not touch. This one here is a timber rattlesnake," he said as he shook the cage and the snake coiled and rattled its tail much more loudly than you would have expected from such a small creature. "It's found mostly in the woods, under felled trees and brush, and this one next to it is a water moccasin, found near streams and springs, obviously. Stay away from both of them." So, of course, Jeremy stepped closer to get a better look as Mama and I backed away. Mama grabbed him by the collar and jerked him away, as Jeremy howled.

But Mr. Denison was unfazed. "This empty cage here," he continued, "is for a copperhead, which blends in so well with our local sandstone cliffs that we haven't been able to catch one yet. My assistant Smokey Woods has been trying to trap one alive, but has been unsuccessful so far. Maybe you'd like to help him, Master Jeremy."

"Oh, yeah!" Jeremy screamed. "Can I, Mama?"

"I don't think so, dear," Mama answered, pulling him along.

Mr. Denison then led us around to the northwest side of the hotel. "There," he said, pointing to a long, two-story cottage across the lawn, "is Memphis Row. We built it originally as a dance hall and billiards room, but, because of our success in attracting guests, we've converted it into thirty-six adult guest rooms. Since many of our guests come from Memphis, we call it Memphis Row."

And there walking down a flower-lined path toward the building, with a cigar in one hand and a bulging, multi-colored carpetbag in the other, was the card-playing man who had snatched Jeremy on the train and called him a brat. Of course, there's no doubt that he's right; Jeremy is definitely a brat. But I still don't like someone else, especially a stranger, calling him that.

"There's the man I told you about," I told Mama, "the one who grabbed Jeremy in the club car."

"I see," was all Mama said.

The manager then led us back across the porch to the middle of the hotel, smiling along the way to the many guests who sat rocking in the porch chairs, reading, smoking, or just enjoying the view. He addressed most of them by name, as we strolled past them. Everything looked and smelled clean and fresh and natural, and I began to understand why they claimed that this place was so healthy.

When we arrived at the stairs to the double-decked, bell-roofed observatory, the manager stopped and pointed to the seventy foot high water tank beneath it, filled, he said, with fifteen thousand gallons of water pumped by a series of elaborate pumps from a big spring, called appropriately enough, but not very imaginatively, "Big Spring," in downtown Huntsville. And under the tank were the bathrooms — all with porcelain-lined tubs, he said — and separate water closets for men and women.

"Then in the south wing, we also have a barber shop, a saloon, a billiards room, and the men's smoking lounge, as well as two ten-pin bowling alleys in a separate building just northeast of here. We also have a new lawn tennis court and croquet, of course, and a complete livery stable in the hotel's annex just southeast of the hotel, with our four-in-hand Tally Ho coaches, trained coach horses, carriages, buggies, two carts, riding horses and ponies — not to mention a well-trained staff of horsemen and guides. If you want to go riding or take a carriage ride, just let Mr. Schrimsher or me know and we'll be happy to arrange it for you. We have nearly twenty miles of well-marked trails for your hiking and riding pleasure."

Mr. Denison then led us up the stairs to the second floor. "We have you in Room Two-seventeen," he said, as we walked down a long hallway bordered on one side by lattice and solid doors to each room. He opened the lattice door to our room and put the key in the lock and opened the tall oak door. "Note the Brussels carpet, and the marble-topped washstand and dresser. The beds for you, Mrs. Franklin, and you, Miss Sophie, are furnished with spring and horsehair mattresses, while Master Jeremy will, I'm sure, enjoy this comfortable cot we have set up for him near the window."

Jeremy scowled, as he tested the firmness of the mattresses by bouncing up and down on them with his rear-end, until Mama caught him by the collar and told him to stop.

"Each room has a call bell, right here," the manager said, as he pointed to a red velvet cord next to the door, "if you need anything at all, just pull it." Which, of course, Jeremy promptly did.

"And in the hall there is a fire hose, if, God forbid, that is needed," Mr. Denison said, ignoring Jeremy.

"This will do nicely," Mama smiled.

"And, finally, here is your door to the upper porch," he said, as he opened the door with a flourish. "Enjoy the view. You're seventeen hundred feet above sea level and about a thousand feet above Huntsville. Enjoy your stay."

Our bags arrived shortly, and, as Mama unpacked them, Jeremy and I stood on the porch and gazed down at the valley below and the Tennessee River glistening in the sun like a slithering, silver snake in the far-off distance to the south. And then on the narrow dirt road between the hotel and the bluff boardwalk, I looked down and saw the most amazing sight of this most amazing day: a fair-skinned boy, in tan canvas work trousers and white cotton shirt, about my age, with a curly mess of brown hair, leading a pretty palomino pony toward the front entrance of the hotel. He was as cocky as a prize fighter; I could tell just by the way he strutted. And, when Jeremy yelled, "Hey, look at that horse," the boy looked up at us and stared and then … smiled, his white teeth gleaming in the afternoon glimmer. And, even though he was much too cocky for my liking, I smiled back.

Sophie Franklin
June 20, 1892

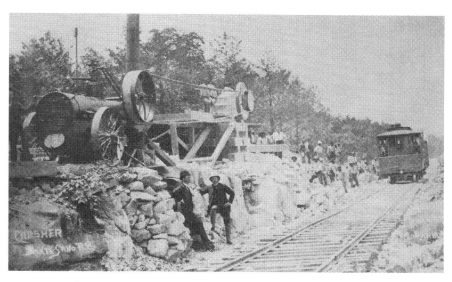

The Monte Sano Railway and Rock Crusher

Brigand's Den

CHAPTER SIX

WHEN MR. DENISON TELLS ME I'm done for the day, I grab an apple to eat from Cook Cazzy in the kitchen and then go looking for Jude in the stable. He isn't there, but Sherm tells me he's taken off down the bluff. If he's going that way, I reckon he's going to one of two places where we like to hide out when no one is telling us what to do, which ain't that often. We've got lots of hideouts, but the ones closest to the stable are just down the bluff below the northwest corner of the mountain top, not too far from the Rison place. They're hard to get to, cause the bluff's so steep right in there, so we ain't usually bothered by no one trying to get us to do something or other.

I walk over to the point and then start scrambling down the bluff until I get to Brigand's Den. It ain't much of a cave, more like a hole in the rocks, but a good place to keep dry when it's raining. But Jude's not there either. I trip over one of my traps that I had forgotten all about as I enter the cave. The trap's door is still open and the bait is gone. So I continue down the hill a little further to Earthquake Glen, which is a little clearing at the foot of this rocky cliff, with a good view of the valley below. And, sure enough, there's old Jude, sitting on a rock, staring out into space.

"What's up?" I ask him.

"Not much," he mutters and spits into the rocks.

"What?"

"Oh, it's just Rogers again," Jude says, shaking his head. "The man tore into Sherm about him feeding the horses too much, and I took up for Sherm. So Rogers tells me to shut up and I walk away. It was either that or I was gonna deck him."

"You want me to talk to Mr. Denison again?" I ask him.

"Nah, it won't do any good. If Rogers is O'Shaughnessy's cousin, there ain't nothing your boss can do about it. Besides my daddy says that I gotta learn to live with an occasional bad boss, if I wanna get along. Life ain't always fair and all that …"

"Yeah, sounds familiar. Seems like grown-ups spend a lot of time puttin' up with a lot of unfairness instead of just doin' something about it."

"What else?"

"You seen the new family in two-seventeen?"

"Uh-huh," I answer. "I can't keep up with 'em all when the hotel's full like it is now."

"I was bringing Shadow around for a guest to go riding this afternoon and this little kid yells at me from the balcony. So I look up and there's this boy and this little peach of a gal up there lookin' down at me. She's just a slip of a thing with olive skin, coal black hair, big, round, brown eyes, and a smile that about knocked me out. I swear, you should've seen her, Smokey; she was somethin' else."

"You know the rule 'bout not gittin' friendly with the guests," I warn him.

"I know," he says, "but it don't hurt to look, does it?"

"Sounds to me like you're interested in more than lookin'."

"Maybe," he says. "Maybe, I am."

Entrance to the O'Shaughnessy Place

The O'Shaughnessy Place

CHAPTER SEVEN

THE NEXT MORNING, Mr. Denison hands me a stuffed white envelope and tells me to deliver it to Colonel O'Shaughnessy at his house. So I take off runnin' across the top of the mountain to his place a couple of miles southeast of the hotel.

Mr. Denison has told me all about his boss and the owner of the Hotel Monte Sano, James O'Shaughnessy. The man is rich. He's got more money than God, Mr. Denison says.

For some reason, I got a head for numbers, so I can remember about all of them that I hear or read. So I know, if Mr. Denison is right, that O'Shaughnessy was born in Dublin, Ireland, in 1843, and then moved to Cincinnati with his parents and his brother Michael in 1846. Both brothers went to a school called St. Xavier's College in Cincinnati and then worked in their family's dry goods store. Both of them landed cushy jobs during the War Between the States, according to Mr. Denison; Michael counted money in the Treasury Department and James pushed papers in the Quartermasters Corp. Michael came out of the Union army a major and James, a colonel. Then, once Reconstruction had begun, they used these titles and their military contacts to make a bunch of money down here in the South where everything was a big mess cause of the War. I've heard them called carpetbaggers and Yankee scoundrels, but Dr. Denison calls them robber barons, but told me not to quote him on that.

Whatever they were, they knew how to invest and take risks and make lots of money. Their warehouse in Nashville was the first one to ship cotton out of Nashville after the war in 1865. And, by 1868, the two brothers had opened a cottonseed oil factory in Nashville, one of the first in the post-war South. By 1871, Mr. Denison said, James had saved up enough money to move to New York, where he married a high-class lady named Lucy Waterbury, the daughter of a well-to-do judge. He started a cottonseed oil refinery in Brooklyn and made even more money, enough to buy forty-three acres of prime development property in Harlem. And he still had enough left over to invest in the new port down in Pensacola, Florida.

Mr. Denison said that, despite all their money, the brothers did have some tough times, like during the Black Friday gold crisis of 1873, but they somehow made it through all that and started expanding again. Brother Michael moved his business in Nashville to Huntsville in 1873, where he saw a chance to further cash in on the broad fields of cotton which covered most of the flatlands of North Alabama in the fall like a fine layer of newly-fallen snow. So, in 1886, he talked James, two men from Memphis, and eighteen local investors into forming a business they called the North Alabama Improvement Company. During the next few years, the partners attracted a bunch of new industries to Huntsville. The O'Shaughnessy brothers' cottonseed oil business was expanded, construction of the Dallas textile mill in East Huntsville was begun, and a broom making company was started. And, to support these businesses, the Improvement Company built a small mill community to house the workers just south of the downtown area.

The Improvement Company advertised Huntsville as the "Queen City of the South." I asked Mr. Denison what the "*King* City of the South" was, but he didn't know for sure; maybe Atlanta, he said, before Sherman burned it down. So they continued to invest, soon owning a lot of downtown Huntsville, including the Huntsville Hotel and the Huntsville Opera House, as well as a few thousand acres in and around Huntsville and on top of Monte Sano.

Mr. Denison said since the early 1800's rich folks from Huntsville have been coming up to Monte Sano in the summer to escape the heat and get away from all the illnesses down along the river, like yellow fever, cholera, and malaria — "the valley of the bad head," the Indians called it. So the Improvement Company decided to take advantage of this reputation for healthiness that was already established and develop a health resort and a place for people to come for summer vacations. By 1887, the Company had bought up most of Monte Sano's plateau, the Monte Sano Turnpike Company, and nearly all of the mountain's western slopes. They picked the land next to the little village of Viduta on the western bluff overlooking Huntsville to be the site of the Hotel Monte Sano.

Mr. Denison said that the Colonel has an apartment at the Waldorf Astoria Hotel in New York City, as well as a fancy estate on Buzzard's Bay in Massachusetts. In 1885, he purchased the Monte Sano summer home built in 1835 by Robert Fearn, Sr., an early Huntsville cotton and real estate broker, whose brother Dr. Thomas Fearn folks say gave the mountain its name, Monte Sano, based on the Italian for mountain, *monte*, and for health, *sanita*.

Unfortunately, the house built by Fearn burned down two years ago. Jude and his daddy helped put out the fire, with the help of some men from Huntsville who rushed up the mountain when they saw the flames. They were able to remove about nine hundred dollars worth of furniture from the house before the fire hose burned in half. So they had resorted to buckets, but by then it was too late and there was not much left of the old house but smoldering ashes.

So O'Shaughnessy rebuilt, and what a rebuilding it was. I've been here a few times before, but each time I come back I'm still amazed by the place. First, you come up to the main entrance that has a stone gatehouse with a cone-shaped roof with wooden fish-scale shingles. The big yard is surrounded by a stone fence with three iron rails across the top about chest high, and there's a heavy wrought iron carriage gate across the road to the right of the gatehouse. It's always unlocked when I've been here, so I just push it open and go right in.

The first thing you see is this tall, tiered concrete vase, about twenty feet tall, covered in ivy. Then a little further down the road, past this lily pond, sitting on a little rise is this big, old mansion of a house. I've heard it called "Castle Delight" and "Mountain Villa," but most people around here just call it the O'Shaughnessy Place. It's huge and sort of looks like the hotel itself, with its two stories, round corner towers, high rooflines, four fancy tall chimneys, a carriage porch with an observation deck, and a detached kitchen with its own root cellar.

I've never been inside, except once, when Colonel O'Shaughnessy was away, and the colored butler Marcus Wilkens showed me around. The house has gas lights just like at the hotel, water lines going to indoor bathrooms covered with fancy ceramic tiles, a wide ornate stairway, stained and leaded glass all over the place, dark oak paneling, and plaster walls throughout.

So today I walk up onto the wide cedar porch which looks like it goes all the way around the house, and I hear a heated argument going on through an open window. Now, Mr. Denison has never directly told me to eavesdrop on anyone, but he has told me that part of my job is to keep my eyes and ears open and report back to him anything I think he should know about what's going on at his hotel. Even though Colonel O'Shaughnessy and a few other investors actually own the hotel, Mr. Denison acts like he does. So I sort of ease up next to the wall, near the window, and listen.

"I'm telling you, Colonel," an old man's voice is exclaiming, "you and your investors are way over-extended and too much in debt. I've seen it a hundred times. You're just one bad season away from disaster."

"You know, Jay, you're getting awfully conservative in your old age. Use to be you were fearless. Now you see trouble around every corner. I may not own as many railroads as you do, but I've been in business for more than twenty-five years now, and I think I know something about making money."

"Maybe so, but you're still blind, old man, to all the things that could go wrong here. Just listen to me. I've got a group of developers from Pierre, South Dakota, who're ready to buy everything you own right now. If you're smart, you'll take the money and run."

"Alright, I know we have a lot going on right now, what with the two hotels, and the opera house, and the debt on the railroad construction," O'Shaughnessy says, "but we're doing okay. We've invested a lot of money, sure, but now we're going to start seeing a real return on it. I know it. I just know. You've seen it, Jay. Why, the hotel is packed. We don't have a vacant room in the house."

"Yeah, but the most you're charging for a couple is thirty-five dollars a week, and you're only open five months out of the year. You need more cash money coming in year round to keep it going."

"We have the hotel in town during the winter."

"Who wants to come to Huntsville in the winter?"

"Business people. Folks from the North wanting to get away from the cold and snow."

"Nonsense. All the businessmen who are interested in Huntsville are already here, and there're a lot nicer places than North Alabama to spend the winter, I guarantee you that. Besides, we're in a boom-bust economy, you know that. And I'm telling you, all the signals point to another bust. The railroads, construction, agriculture are all down and they're going to go down farther, mark my words."

"I'm not so sure you know what you're talking about, Jay. Maybe things up north are in trouble, but we still have a lot of room for expansion down here. I have very high hopes."

"I know you do, but you need more than hope, you need cash coming in on a regular basis. If I were you, I wouldn't bet on cashing in on all these expensive investments. My money's on this World's Columbian Exposition in Chicago next year. That's where all the tourists are going to be going, not down here to some backwater hotel in the piney woods of Alabama."

"We'll see," O'Shaughnessy says.

"Just hear these boys from South Dakota out. Think of all the things that could go wrong and ruin your business in a New York minute. Why, what if someone finds a cure for yellow fever, then there goes all your southern clientele just like that. Or tuberculosis. I probably wouldn't be down here right now if someone had figured out how to cure that. What if you have another train wreck and someone gets killed this time? What would that do to your business?"

"Jay, you're being crazy now. If I ran my business on 'what-if's', I'd be too afraid to turn around."

"Okay, Colonel, whatever you say. But if one drunk hotel guest stumbles off the side of this mountain and kills himself, you know who to call."

The Hotel Monte Sano

At this point, I think I've heard enough, so I slowly back away from the window and tip-toe to the front door, where Wilkens the colored butler answers my knock and takes the envelope from Mr. Denison. I'm not exactly sure what the argument I've just heard means, but I bet Mr. Denison will be glad I heard it.

CHAPTER EIGHT

IT DIDN'T TAKE LONG *for Ma to find out who the head of the Lawrence County Alabama Home Guard was, the man who had led the band of horsemen who had killed Junior's pa and brother John. She knew pretty much everyone in the Black Dutch community around Moulton, and many were beholden to her in one way or another, owing to her knowledge of Cherokee medicine and traditional Indian midwifery.*

So, on a cloudy, windy night in September, 1865, she and Junior, just twelve-years-old at the time, and his older brother Mack rode into Moulton to pay a visit to the home of Dr. Andrew Kaiser.

They left their wagon and the mule that was pulling it tied in an oak grove just outside of town on Market Street and walked about half a mile to the doctor's house that set alone in the middle of a broad field of high, full-bolled cotton. Ma gave Junior a burlap bag to carry. While Mack stood guard at the front door, Junior and Ma crept from window to window until they found the open bedroom window at the rear of the white clapboard house and peered in at the sleeping couple. Ma propped her shotgun on the windowsill and aimed it at Dr. Kaiser's head.

"Wake up, Doctor," Ma whispered. "Wake up, sleepy head."

When the doctor did not stir, Ma raised her voice and repeated her request.

"Come on, Doctor. Time to rise and shine. Time to meet your maker."

Finally, as Ma's voice grew louder and louder, the doctor awoke in the dim light, fumbled for his spectacles on the bedside table, found them and put them on, and then glared with alarm at Ma and the shotgun pointed at him. "Remember me?" Ma asked.

The doctor, confused and groggy, shook his head, and said no.

"I'm Jenny Brooks. You and your men murdered my husband Willis and my son John out on Whitman Creek not too long ago. Ring any bells?"

The doctor started to rise, but Ma told him to stay put or she would blow his brains out. Then the doctor's wife woke up, saw Ma and her shotgun, and gasped.

"You scream," Ma warned her, "and you're both dead."

"What do you want?" the doctor asked her.

"Just the names of the men who are in the Lawrence County Home Guard," Ma told him.

"I can't do that."

"Then I'll shoot you," Ma said as she crouched and aimed the shotgun.

"Don't," Mrs. Kaiser begged, "I'll tell you."

"No," Kaiser ordered, "don't tell her."

"Stand up, Doctor," Ma ordered. "Put your hands on your head and walk slowly to the wall in front of me."

The doctor, in his long white nightshirt, did as he was told.

"Now, Mrs. Kaiser, give me the names or I will kill your husband."

"No," the doctor said.

"Jeff Hogan," the doctor's wife blubbered from her bed.

"Keep going," Ma ordered.

"No!" protested the doctor, as he stepped forward.

Ma pulled the trigger, shattering the silence of the night, as well as Dr. Kaiser's barrel chest, his flesh and blood and splintered bones splattering wildly against the wall and throughout the room. Mrs. Kaiser did not scream, only turned her head into the pillow and began to sob uncontrollably.

"The names," Ma demanded, as she reloaded the shotgun. "Write them down, Junior. There's paper and pencil in your bag.

"Bob South," the doctor's wife stammered, " Mack Gosey … Jim Smith … Sherm Williams … Hue Lagion … Bill Weams."

Junior wrote them down, spelling them the best he could.

"Now, hand me the ax that's in your bag," Ma told Junior, as she crawled through the open window into the bloody bedroom. Now, Junior had seen his ma perform many acts of violence around the farm. She routinely wrung the necks of chickens that were to be fried for supper, she castrated calves before they were put out to pasture, and she effortlessly butchered hogs to take to market. So Ma and death and blood were no strangers; even so, Junior was not prepared for what she did next. She calmly walked over to Dr. Kaiser's prone body and began chopping his neck with the ax. Blood and gore flew on Ma and all over the floor, while the dead man's wife continued to moan and cry face down in her pillow. Junior was shocked and frightened, but he could not look away. It took quite an effort on Ma's part to separate the doctor's head from the rest of his body. But when she had finally severed the stubborn neck bone, the head fell loose and rolled across the pine floor to the window where Junior stood agape.

"Hold your bag open," Ma told Junior.

Ma walked over to the window, reached out, and dropped the bloody ax into the burlap bag. Then, with her blood-soaked right hand, she picked up Dr. Kaiser's slippery, disembodied head by its greasy black hair and dropped it into the bag, which nearly slipped out of Junior's grasp with its surprising new weight.

When they arrived back home on Whitman Creek, Ma told Junior to clean the ax at the well and then to chop her a sturdy limb from the hickory tree where the guardsmen had hanged Pa. While he was doing that, Ma told Mack to fill the cast-iron cauldron in the backyard with water and then to start a fire under it. After she had carved a deep notch in the hickory stave and the water in the cauldron was boiling, she took the doctor's bloody head from the burlap bag and dropped it into the boiling water.

Later, as the sun was beginning to rise the next morning and the fire under the cauldron had died to ashes, Ma took a shovel and scooped the head from the cauldron. By then, all the flesh had boiled away, and all that was left was a clean, white skull — its wide, dark eye holes, staring blankly — its gleaming teeth, sharp and gumless. She deposited

51

it in the grass and told Junior to fetch a saw from the barn. With the saw, she carefully sawed off the doctor's lower jaw, threw it to the dogs, and then carried the remainder of the skull into the kitchen.

Junior followed her, entranced by the macabre ceremony.

"What in the world are you doing with that, Ma?" Junior asked, as Ma carefully balanced the naked skull upside down in a bowl on the counter next to the sink and pump.

"Why, I got myself a new wash basin," she smiled.

A Room at the Hotel Monte Sano

Tea on the Hotel Monte Sano Porch

CHAPTER NINE

IT WAS TURNING INTO A WET SUMMER in North Alabama, and on Monte Sano it felt like a sultry, sloppy rain forest, the moisture permeating everything like a soppy sponge. When it stormed, no one wanted to ride or be outside, so Jude and the others who worked in the stable repaired tack, white-washed stalls, and cleaned and polished the coaches and carriages, until supper time.

And then, after supper, they played penny-ante poker or dominoes in an empty stall. On the second night of the lingering storm, as lightning cracked, and rain pelted the stable's tin roof, Jude, Waya, Ivan, and Sherm sat around an old wooden table and played poker. They were well into their fifth game, with Sherm winning most of the games so far this evening, when a stranger sauntered into the stable. As he got closer, Jude recognized him as the big, bearded guest who had arrived on the same day as the new family in Room Two-seventeen.

"You mind if I join you?" he asked, as he removed his Panama hat and shook the rain off it onto the concrete floor. "Ain't no one in the men's smoking lounge or the bowling alley tonight. They're all at some dance. I ain't much for dancin' myself. Poker's more my game, and the man at the front desk said I might find a game over here."

"Sure," Ivan said, as he stood up. "Sherm's about cleaned me out already, so I'm gonna quit for the night. You can take my place."

"Sure y'all don't mind?"

"Nah, have a seat," Waya said. "Ain't much else to do in this rain."

"My name's Bradley Comstock," the man announced, offering his hand, which had unusually long fingers, to the horsemen. "Most folks call me Com."

They all introduced themselves, and the man unbuttoned his jacket and sat down in Ivan's chair. Jude glimpsed a copper Derringer pistol in a black, leather holster on the left side of the man's belt. "What's the game?" Comstock asked.

"Five-card stud," Sherm answered.

"Okay, deal 'em," their guest said. "What's the ante?"

"We usually play a penny ante," Jude told him.

"Just a penny, huh? Ain't much."

"We ain't got much," Sherm told him.

Everybody anted up. Waya dealt the hand. Everyone checked their cards. Jude asked for two. Sherm wanted three. Comstock took one. And Waya folded.

"I raise y'all a nickel," the new man said after checking his cards.

Jude had three two's, so he bet a nickel. Sherm pushed five pennies into the pot and flipped his cards — a pair of aces and a pair of eights. Comstock turned his cards — four kings. It continued like that, with Comstock winning most of the hands, but always winning the hands he dealt himself. Jude and Waya were soon wiped out of the small caches they had come to play with. Only Sherm and Comstock remained. Sherm won a few hands he dealt himself, but Comstock was systematically wiping him out. Finally, when Sherm was down to his last few pennies, Comstock adroitly shuffled the deck, and, just before he began to deal, laid the deck on the table for Sherm to cut. Sherm reached over and put his right hand on top of the cards. "Do you mind if I take a look at these?" he asked Comstock, who squinted hard through his cigar smoke at Sherm.

"Are you suggestin' what I think you're suggestin'?" Comstock asked.

"Ain't suggestin' nothing," Sherm said. "I just wanna see the cards, before I cut them."

Comstock's left hand moved fast and the little pistol was out and pointed at Sherm's heart before Jude or anyone else could stop him. "If you think I've been cheatin', just say so," he growled, cocking the gun.

"You seem to be winnin' very consistently when you deal," Sherm said with a slight tremor in his voice.

The new man looked down at the deck of cards lying on the table and then stared into Sherm's eyes. He held the little gun steady.

"You can go to hell, my friend," Comstock finally said, as he pushed the pile of pennies in front of him across the table and into Sherm's lap. "I don't want you're lousy pennies. And, as far as I'm concerned, you ain't worth shootin'."

And with that Comstock stood, uncocked his pistol and returned it to its holster, buttoned his black jacket, turned, and marched out of the stable.

Lover's Nest Gazebo and Lily Lake

CHAPTER TEN

A FEW DAYS LATER, when the rain had finally stopped, Smokey, out of breath, ran into the stable and found Jude in a back stall, shoveling manure, as usual, into an old, wooden wheelbarrow. "Guess who wants to go riding?" Smokey asked Jude.

"Who?"

"Your little sweetheart in two-seventeen, that's who."

"You're kidding?"

"Nope, her mother sashayed right into Mr. Denison's office first thing this morning and asked him to arrange a horse and a guide for her to see the sites around the mountain while she's takin' care of her son who somehow hit a croquet ball into a yellow-jackets' nest and got stung all over himself. So Mr. Denison sent me over here to fix it up. She wants to go straight-away."

"Have you talked to Rogers yet?" Jude asked.

"Not yet."

"Smokey …"

"Wait a minute," Smokey replied. "I know what you're thinkin', and I ain't gonna do it."

"Smokey …"

"No, there's no way I'm gonna fix it so's you're her guide. You'd just git yourself in trouble, and you know it."

"Smokey … you know I'd do it for you."

"No way, Jude, I ain't havin' no part of it."

"All you have to do is tell Rogers that the guest has requested me as her guide. He won't know the difference."

"But …"

"You know that new fishing pole I got for Christmas … Think of all the fish you could catch with that."

"Oh, Jude, please …"

"It's all yours. All you have to do is have a word with Rogers."

"Well … okay, but only under one condition."

"What?"

"You, gotta promise me, you won't git involved with this gal, cause, for sure, both of us would be in trouble then."

"I promise. Now go talk to Rogers, pleeease."

"You swear on the Bible you won't start somthin' with this gal?"

"Yeah, yeah. Now go!"

When Rogers walked back to tell Jude to saddle up Shadow and Blaze for him and a guest, Jude tried to look as surprised as Rogers seemed to be about the request. "Why would a guest want your sad ass as a guide?" he asked, shaking his head, his right eye beginning to twitch.

"Beats me," Jude lied.

"Well, beats me too, but I ain't gonna argue with 'em. So hurry up and get over there before I change my mind and send someone else."

Jude did as he was told. When he had tied the horses to the hitching post in front of the hotel, he hurried into the lobby and found his father on duty at the front desk. "What are you doing here?" he asked his son.

"Mr. Rogers wants me to take a guest riding today. A Miss Franklin, he said."

"Well, well, so you and Mr. Rogers are getting along better then, I assume?"

"For the time being, anyway. Where is she?"

"Oh, she'll be down presently. Just hold your horses," the elder Schrimsher laughed. "Listen, Jude, seriously, if Mr. Rogers is going to trust you with this responsibility, you have to make sure you do a good job. Be a gentleman and show her the sites, but be very careful with her. She's very little, and, even though her mother says she's an experienced rider, we have no idea how experienced."

"Okay. Don't worry, I'll be careful."

"Good. Now, go to the kitchen and get a basket lunch for y'all and then go wait with your horses. I'll go get her. Her mother and brother are in Doc Duffield's office seeing about his bee stings. The poor kid's legs are covered with 'em and he's been squealing like a stuck pig."

Jude found Cook Cazzy, a former slave, in the kitchen, slicing potatoes. She was a big, aproned, colored woman who never seemed to be at rest. He asked her if she would prepare a lunch basket for a guest and him. "Sure," she said, wiping her hands on a towel and then smothering Jude with a big hug. "Any special requests?"

"No. Everything you make is great."

He wasn't lying either. Even though Chef Conner was in charge of the kitchen, Jude thought Cook Cazzy's cooking was the best he had ever tasted.

For a while last summer, Smokey had been infatuated with Cook Cazzy's pretty granddaughter Ella, who on Sundays would take an excursion train up the mountain from her house on Dallas Street to visit her grandmother and later Smokey. She was just as smart as she was pretty, and she and Smokey would take long walks in the woods where Ella would collect the herbs that her grandmother had taught her about: black snakeroot for rheumatism and arthritis, mullein for fever, dandelion for tea that was good for the blood. But some time during the winter Ella had found another boyfriend and had informed Smokey that she didn't think they should be alone together any more, especially after the ardent kisses they had shared at the end of last summer.

Jude secretly admired Smokey for his ease with girls. Smokey always seemed to know what to say to them and how to act around them. And the girls flocked to him. Jude, on the other hand, despite his confidence in other matters, like tending horses and playing baseball, was shy around girls. Unlike Smokey, he had never had a girlfriend or even come close to having one. He could barely carry on a conversation with a girl, let alone charm one. He didn't even know where to begin. So he was a little anxious about taking this girl riding. Maybe it wasn't such a good idea after all. What could he possibly say to her? But she was so pretty, and it was too late now anyway.

The Hotel Monte Sano

After Cook Cazzy had prepared the picnic basket, Jude waited and waited with the horses in the hot morning sun. It was true that it was anywhere between five and fifteen degrees cooler on Monte Sano than it was in the valley below, but, if you were in the sun this time of year, it could still be stifling. He had to wonder how uncomfortable she was, as she walked toward him, in her heavy, multi-layered, blue skirt and puffy, long-sleeve, white blouse. He smiled and helped her up onto Shadow's sidesaddle. Holding her elbow, he realized how extremely light and slight she was. He imagined that he enjoyed a glimpse of her ankle when she stepped into the stirrup, but it was unlikely with the high-cut, buttoned boots that she was wearing.

They rode north from the hotel on Prospect Drive, the carriage road along the western bluff. Jude led the way, but he could tell by the rhythm of Shadow's even gait behind him that she knew how to ride. They stopped at Grand View on the northwest tip of the plateau and peered out across the broad valley below. A wispy, purple morning mist still hung over Huntsville, making the town look like a fuzzy, slightly out-of-focus fairyland.

"It's beautiful," she said.

"Yeah, you are," he stammered. "I mean … yeah, it's real pretty."

"What's your name?" she asked in a gentle voice.

"Jude. What's yours?"

"Sophie," she answered.

"Where are you from?"

"Schenectady, New York. My dad works for an electric company there. Where do you live?"

"Here," Jude answered. "My daddy and I live in a house on the other side of the mountain during the winter. We have a little farm over there. We take care of most of the summer houses up here when the city folks move back into town during the winter months. And since they built this hotel a few years ago, both my daddy and I've been working here while it's open in the summer time. I stay in the stable cause it's closer than our house, and I like being around the horses."

"How many people live on the mountain?"

"Well," Jude answered, "during the summer, maybe fifty or so families, around three-hundred and fifty people, including servants, all told, scattered around the summit in cottages, mostly on this side of the mountain, but in the winter, only a handful."

"What do they call it?"

"Viduta," Jude answered. "A doctor named Thomas Fearn and his brothers Robert and George started a little health colony up here around 1827, and by 1833 they were calling it Viduta."

"Viduta? That's a funny name."

"Yeah, they told us in school that it comes from the Spanish for 'life': *vida*. I guess because it's supposed to be so healthy up here."

They rode on along the northern bluff, across the plateau, side by side, on the muddy carriage road. The flat top of the mountain is shaped roughly like a fat, jagged horseshoe, with the northern end curving gently along the toe of the shoe and the two heals jutting out to the south. As they rode along the northern perimeter, Jude tried desperately to think of something to ask her, but he was just too timid and tongue-tied to think of anything. So they rode in silence, as a red-tailed hawk circled slowly above them in the cloudless sky.

"What about your mother?" she finally asked him.

"Oh, she's dead. She died when I was born, sixteen years ago in January."

"I'm sorry."

"Oh, it's okay … for me anyway. Cook Cazzy, who works in the kitchen, her daughter Eliza had a daughter Ella who was born around the time I was, so Eliza was my wet nurse up until the time I could eat solid food and Daddy could take care of me. So I never did know my mother, but it's been hard for my daddy, I think. I can tell when he gets quiet sometimes that he's thinking about her."

They rode east and Jude pointed out the summer cottages of the Risons, the Newmans, the Halseys, the Coopers, and then they rode down the bluff about a quarter of a mile, through a grove of basswood, dogwood, and oak, to Cold Spring. Jude dismounted and helped Sophie down from her sidesaddle, holding her hand and elbow. He tied the horses to a nearby tulip tree and fetched water for them from the spring in two of the wooden buckets that were neatly stacked next to the pump.

"Let me show you this tree," Jude said, as he led her to a squat tree with tiny leaves and branches filled with sharp thorns. "It's a chittamwood tree, and they say it grows in the United States only here and in southern Illinois. Of course, Monte Sano supposedly has a hundred and ninety-six different kinds of trees. But this chittamwood is supposed to be really good for making furniture. In fact, it says in the Bible that they used it to make parts of the Tabernacle and the Ark of the Covenant. There's a Negro man who lives on Adams Avenue in Huntsville named Jake Fulgham who can make about anything out of wood, and we still use a chittamwood chest he made for my mother."

Cold Spring was enclosed in an intricate, wooden stave hut, with a small bench beside it, leaning against a tall pin oak tree. Jude and Sophie drank from the spring and then strolled to a gazebo with a cone-shaped roof that rested just a few yards uphill. From there, they had a good view of the toll road and railroad tracks that wound through the hollow below.

"The water from this spring is supposed to be some of the purest and coldest in Alabama," Jude said. "Around fifty-five degrees, they say. They pump it from here to the dining room at the hotel. One of the first white men to live up here was a man named John Martin who built a house right down there in 1815. He piped the water from this spring to his house in hollow, red cedar logs and even carved a bathtub out of limestone to collect the water and bathe in. Some say it was the first indoor bathtub in America."

"It must have made for an awfully cold bath," Sophie said.

"Yeah, can you imagine jumping naked into an ice-cold stone tub in the middle of winter?"

"I'd rather stay dirty," Sophie said.

After the horses had been watered and rested, they mounted them again. Jude made a step by clasping his hands together, and Sophie placed her right foot in it and balanced herself with a hand on Jude's shoulder, as he hoisted her up into the sidesaddle.

"There's a little cave just down the bluff from here called Cold Spring Cave," Jude told her. "Would you like to see it?"

"Sure," she answered. "Let's go."

So they rode down the trail a few hundred yards, across the Monte Sano Turnpike and the railroad, where they stopped and dismounted. Jude told Sophie that the trail was too steep for the horses, so they tied them to a magnolia tree.

Jude removed a kerosene lantern from Blaze's saddlebag and led Sophie down the narrow, rocky path to the cave entrance, a dark, forbidding hole about six feet across, in the side of the mountain. Jude lit the lantern and descended first.

"Are you sure about this?" Sophie asked, hesitating at the cave's entrance.

"It's steep and slippery. Just be careful. Stay near the rocks on the wall and follow me."

"Okay, if you say so."

Jude led her down the steep hole into the cave's cold darkness. There were a lot of rocks and mud on the cave's floor, and the lantern didn't produce that much light, so they stumbled slowly down into the wet, gloomy tunnel. Jude held the lantern up toward the cave's dome which became increasingly high as they moved deeper into the pit. Many gray, imposing stalactites decorated the ceiling. They continued on, with the acrid smell of the lantern in the damp air and the sound of dripping water growing louder and louder, as they crept forward. Then Jude held the lantern out in front of them and they saw the source of the water. A high, stone waterfall blocked their path, but the lantern was not strong enough for them to see its top — water just trickled down the smooth, orange wall from somewhere above them into the dark rocks at their feet, like a pretty polished curtain, blocking their way.

"That's all there is," Jude told her. "The cave ends here."

"Wow!" she said.

So he led her back up the muddy trail toward the entrance, where they could see the bright light of day flowing in. About halfway up, Sophie slipped and fell into Jude's backside, bringing him down with her onto the cave's wet, sloping floor. Jude almost lost the lantern, but was able to hang onto it, just barely, as he fell onto the rocks. He turned over with Sophie still on him, holding the lantern away from her clothes and hair.

"Sorry," she said, as she rolled off of him.

"I'm not," Jude said, thinking how soft and warm she had felt lying briefly there on top of him, smelling of smoke and lilac. "But are you alright?"

"I think so."

Jude helped her up and they crawled the few remaining feet up and out into the dry, bright light of day.

Their clothes were muddy and soiled, but they were both smiling. Jude extinguished the lantern, and they climbed back up the trail to the horses. Jude helped Sophie back up on Shadow. They backtracked to Cold Spring and then followed the sign on an oak tree that read: "Cemetery Route — Horse Services Procured at the Annex to the Hotel — Keep to the Right." So they did, riding up the bluff until they reached a small cemetery at the summit.

"There used to be a school for girls up here years ago," Jude said, as he helped Sophie down from Shadow. "A Methodist minister named Reverend James Rowe and his wife Malinda opened a boarding school called the Monte Sano Female Seminary in 1830. They taught the classics, science, English, French, Latin, drawing, painting, and, something every young lady should know, needle work and embroidery. But it didn't last very long. Reverend Rowe closed it down when Malinda died unexpectedly in 1833. Look, here's her grave stone right here."

They both knelt before one of the two gray, eight-foot obelisks, and Sophie read aloud the carved inscription:

> *M. A. Rowe*
> *Wife of Rev. Jas. Rowe*
> *Died Nov. 18, 1833*
> *In the hope of Resurrection in Christ*
> *She rests from her Labor*
> *And her works shall follow her*

"How did she die?" Sophie asked.

"No one remembers," Jude answered. "Some say she suffered from rheumatism and others believe she may have died in childbirth, like my mother. But, who knows, maybe you'll have a chance to ask her yourself. They say her ghost still roams the mountain, looking for her husband and two young sons who moved to Ohio soon after her death."

"You're kidding?"

"No," Jude said. "I've never seen her, but lots of others have."

"I'm not sure I believe in ghosts."

"No? Well, keep your eyes open anyway. You never know. Some hotel guests say they've seen her wandering around the halls in the hotel late at night."

They rode southeast across the plateau, over the railroad tracks, past Laura's View Station and the summer homes of the families of Morris Bernstein, Robert Herstein, Issac Shiffman, and Oscar Goldsmith, and then picked up the old Choctaw Indian Trail along the bluff to Landon and Henrietta Carter's house and the falls of Chalybeate Spring nearby. From above the spring they had a sweeping view of McKay Hollow and the wooded cliffs that lined it.

"What is chalybeate?" Sophie asked, as they looked out over the dense forest below.

"It's a type of mineral water, supposedly containing iron salts and having all kinds of curing effects for people who are run-down and thin-blooded. Want a taste?"

"No, that's okay."

"It has a sort of a metallic taste, but it's not bad."

They continued along the old trail, at the top of the bluff, with the leaves of buckeye, oak, and hickory trees, playing peekaboo with their view of Big Cove far off in the distance below. Finally, the trail widened as they caught sight of the open gates to the O'Shaughnessy's place. They rode into the empty yard and past the ivy-covered urn to a small, round lake partially covered in blooming white and green lily pads and multi-colored cannas.

They stopped at water's edge, dismounted, and watched the horses drink from the shallow pool. After they had had their fill, Jude tied the horses to a sweet gum tree, removed the picnic basket that he had tied to the back of Blaze's saddle and led Sophie to the gazebo next to the lake. They climbed the stairs to the roofed platform, with fish-scale shingles just like the ones on the gatehouse they had passed earlier. There was a lot of fancy lattice woodwork, but it didn't block their view of the water and the two arched foot bridges, one at each end of the lake.

They sat next to each other on the wooden bench with the picnic basket between them. Jude began unpacking it.

"Are you hungry?" he asked.

"Ravenous!"

"Good, let's see what we have here. Cook Cazzy is the best cook in Alabama, and she made this, so it should be good. Looks like some sort of meatloaf or pate thing here, and then some sandwiches too, cheese and olive, I think, and potato salad, two apples, and a jar of lemonade."

"What a feast," Sophie said, taking the plate from Jude. "Tell me about this place. It's so beautiful and quiet. All you can hear are the birds singing."

"Well, Colonel O'Shaughnessy lives in a big ol' house just on the other side of this little lake. He owns the hotel, along with some other investors, and a lot of land and other stuff around here. Apparently, he took this old fish pond and turned it into what he calls Lily Lake, something like the lily pond that this famous French painter named Claude Monet painted a bunch of pictures of. They call this place we're sitting in the Lover's Nest Gazebo, and that path around the lake that's lined with rocks and roses is called Flirtation Path."

"How romantic," Sophie said.

"Yes," was the only thing that Jude could think to say to that.

"Tell me about what it's like to live here on this remote mountain in North Alabama."

So Jude told her everything he could think of about Monte Sano and himself — hesitantly at first, but then more freely as she listened intently and prompted him with occasional questions — about their farm at the other end of the mountain, and the coal mines and the lumber camps on the western side, his daily horseback trips to Huntsville to go to school in the winter, his love of horses and other animals, his daddy who was the head bellman at the hotel, his friend Smokey who knew about everything that went on at the hotel, and the other men who worked in the stable, including his arch enemy and boss, A.D. Rogers.

And then he asked Sophie to tell him about Schenectady and her life in New York, where he had never been. So she told him about her aloof, but loving father who was some sort of big-wig manager of a company called Edison General Electric, and how big and bustling their town was, and how her mother babied her little brother Jeremy, and what a pain he was, and how much she liked riding horses with her friends Willa and Susan and how much she missed them and her father back in New York.

By the time they had finished their lunches and their stories the sun was beginning to touch the tops of the trees on the western slope of the mountain. So they packed up their dirty dishes and descended the steps of the gazebo. After Jude had shown Sophie where the outhouse was, they returned to the horses grazing quietly in the shade.

"Wanna race?" Sophie asked, as Jude bent over to again form a two-handed step-up for her to mount Shadow.

"What?"

"Do you wanna race me and Shadow around the lake, on Flirtation Path? There's nobody around to run over. It'll be fun."

"But, it wouldn't be fair. You riding sidesaddle and me riding astride."

"That's true," Sophie said. "So why don't you take Shadow's saddle off, and I'll ride bareback."

"Astride?"

"Sure, why not? If you can do it, why can't I?"

"But ..."

"Do you want me to take the saddle off?"

"No," Jude said, "I'll do it. It's just that ... if you're sure ... but it seems dangerous."

"I've ridden bareback plenty of times at home. The Indians did it all the time. It's no big deal."

"But …"

"What? You've never seen a girl ride astride before?"

"No," Jude admitted, "I haven't. It just doesn't seem … right."

"Why not?"

"I don't know. Are you sure you wanna do this? What if you fall?"

"I won't. Don't worry," Sophie reassured him. "Maybe you're just afraid I'll beat you."

"Okay, if you say so," Jude said, shaking his head. If there was one thing he couldn't resist, it was a challenge — and, of course, the insistence of a pretty girl who was standing right there in front of him, practically daring him.

So he removed the sidesaddle and leaned it against the trunk of the sweet gum tree.

"Give me a boost up," Sophie said, as she lifted the hems of her skirts.

This time there was no doubt about what Jude saw, and it wasn't an imagined fleeting glimpse of an ankle, but instead a pair of pale, slim calves and the ruffled bottoms of a pair of white, cotton bloomers that barely covered her knees. With her hems raised, she stepped into Jude's clasped hands. Then she dropped her skirts, and firmly grasped Shadow's mane, as Jude hoisted her up. Once astride, Sophie leaned forward and flipped the back of her skirts out from under her rump, splaying them, blue on top and white petticoats beneath out across the horse's broad haunch.

"Ready," she said, smiling down to Jude.

So he mounted Blaze and maneuvered him alongside Shadow.

"On three," she said, as she grasped the reins and leaned forward over Shadow's neck. "One, two, three!"

They were off. Now, Jude knew that Sophie rode the faster horse. He had raced all the riding horses in the stable with Smokey or Waya when Mr. Rogers was in town, but he still wasn't prepared for Sophie's speedy break. She had Shadow out in front by a length before they even reached the first bridge. Then on the backstretch it became no contest, as Sophie pressed the palomino into full stride. All Jude could see then was Sophie's skirts flying and her long black hair, now loose from its prim bun, fluttering freely in the wind farther and farther in front of him.

By the time they had crossed the second bridge and turned into the homestretch, Sophie was almost a furlong ahead and Jude had no chance of catching her. She was already reining Shadow in and turning him around when Jude and Blaze crossed the spot where they had begun.

The Hotel Monte Sano Lobby

CHAPTER ELEVEN

DEAR DIARY,

OH, WHAT A DAY! My rear-end is sore from riding, and I should be upset at the trouble we caused, but my heart is happy. If I thought the day we arrived was amazing, this day was even more so. The cocky boy who I saw from the porch that day turned out to be the guide who showed me around Monte Sano on horseback today. And, believe me, he was even more amazing up close, and not so cocky, than he was at a distance, looking like some sort of young Greek god and smelling of horsehide and leather, and shy and oh so full of himself, all at the same time.

After he showed me the local sites, we had a picnic lunch, and I beat him in a horse race. I know I shouldn't have done that. Mama has told me to be kind to men, because they're so much more vulnerable than they appear to be, but I couldn't help myself, and the horse I was riding was so much faster than his.

As we rode back from the little lake that we raced around, I talked Jude — that's the boy's name — into letting me see the stable where he works and where they keep all the hotel's horses and carriages. He didn't want to show me unless his boss, a man named Rogers, wasn't there, because he said that if this man saw how pretty I was, he would suspect that Jude had somehow arranged for him to be my guide. He actually said that, that I was pretty. Funny, I never see myself that way, but I'm really glad he does. I'm too little and too plain and too talkative. Anyway, I asked Jude if he really had arranged to be my guide, and he just smiled and said he wasn't going to answer that question, which told me he had. I don't know how, but I'm glad he did.

To make sure this man Rogers was not in the stable, Jude had us dismount and quietly lead our horses to a little cedar grove near the stable. Then Jude had me hold the horses in the gathering twilight while he crept around the stable, trying to see or hear if Rogers was in there. That's when the trouble began. When Jude had disappeared on the other side of the stable, I heard a man's angry voice from inside. He was yelling at someone, and he was not happy.

"You'll do as I say, Sherm, or I'll have your damn neck. There are no other horses available right now, and Mister Denison wants that sad ass Jude and that girl found before dark — no matter what. Do you understand me?"

"Yeah, I understand alright," another man's voice said, "but I ain't gonna ride a lame horse outta this barn tonight or any other night. I'll go on foot. I'll try to find another mount to borrow, but I ain't gonna put an injured horse through that agony, no matter what you say or do."

"Then get out there on foot and find 'em," the man yelled. "And if you don't, before sundown, I'll personally throttle you myself. Now go!"

As this tall man, apparently Sherm, appeared from the stable door, Jude came from around the corner of the stable and led him into the woods to me. "You're in big trouble," Sherm whispered to Jude and me. "This here gal's mama is fit to be tied. Where've y'all been?"

"It doesn't matter," Jude said. "If you'll take these horses back to the stable, I'll walk Miss Franklin back to the hotel and explain it all to her mother."

"Okay, if you say so," Sherm said, "but I hope you've got a good explanation, cause there's a lot of upset folks around here this evenin'."

It really was getting dark by this time, and I was afraid for Jude, so, as we walked back through the woods to the hotel, I reached over and grabbed his hand, which was about twice the size of mine. He squeezed my hand tightly, but I didn't mind. I just wanted us to be touching, like we had in the cave. When we got close to the hotel, we unclasped our hands and Jude said, "Let me do the talking."

"Okay," I agreed, since, for once, I didn't have a clue to what to say.

As we walked up the stairs to the hotel's front door, I whispered to him, "No matter what happens, promise me we'll somehow see each other again, okay?"

"I promise," he said and smiled the best smile I've ever seen in my entire life.

The rest was not pretty. When we got back to the hotel's lobby, Jude's daddy took him straight to the manager's office, and Mr. Denison firmly ushered me up to our room where Mama was waiting and weeping, as Jeremy bounced merrily on the bed, until he fell off and began crying again.

Now she and Jeremy are finally asleep, after I explained to Mama that nothing bad had happened and that it was all my fault that we were so late, because I wanted to see so much and dawdled along the way. I told her that Jude had tried to hurry me along and that he bore absolutely no blame for our tardiness whatsoever, and I pleaded for her to let Jude guide me again on another tour as soon as possible. Mama just looked tired and said, "We'll see about that. Now go to bed."

Sophie Franklin
June 23, 1892

CHAPTER TWELVE

JUNIOR'S MA WAS BORN *Louisa Elisabeth Jane Bates on January 22, 1826, in Jefferson County, Kentucky. She married Willis Brooks, who was twenty-one years her senior, in 1840, when the young bride was just fourteen. By 1850, the couple was living along Whitman Creek in rural Lawrence County, Alabama, with their three young children. Aunt Jenny, as she was known, bore six more children in subsequent years, with eighteen years separating the first from the last.*

Junior's pa Willis was a sometimes saddler, farmer, bootlegger, hunter, and a full-time, full-out rascal. His wife Jenny was a half-breed Cherokee Indian with black hair, dark skin, and blue eyes. She was a midwife in the area and tried to help her sick neighbors the best she could with her knowledge of Cherokee medicine. Other than that, she kept to herself and expected her neighbors to do the same. One time Junior watched her pull a thick wad of bills from her skirts to pay for provisions at a dry goods store in Moulton. When the nosy clerk asked her about the amount of money she was carrying, Mama snapped back, "I pay myself twenty dollars a month to mind my own business! I suggest you do the same!"

After Aunt Jenny had shot and beheaded Dr. Kaiser, the head of the Lawrence County Alabama Home Guard, the doctor's widow had warned the other guardsmen that she had named them to her husband's killer. So most of them had scattered.

The Lawrence County sheriff had tried to convince the doctor's widow to identify her husband's killer. But scared speechless by the ferocity of her husband's demise and fearing the vengeance Aunt Jennie and her family might exact on her, she refused to discuss the matter with the sheriff or anyone else.

The two guardsmen who remained in the area were soon shot dead by Jenny herself. Over the next several years, her sons tracked down the rest. One by one, they killed them all. Bob South was strangled in Hartselle by one of the bullwhips that he so much loved to brandish. Hue Lagio, bloated and floating face down, was fished out of the Sipsey River near Double Springs. Jeff Hogan ate a generous wedge of the apple pie that his wife had baked and left on the window sill to cool at their home in Decatur before he keeled over and died, apparently of arsenic poisoning. And Mack Gosey was found by his wife hanging by his neck from the limb of a shagbark hickory tree in their backyard in Cullman.

Jenny and her sons were never named in any of these killings. Either there was insufficient evidence, or, when the law had become too suspicious, the sons had just disappeared, sometimes into the surrounding wilderness or into a remote gorge in Dismals Canyon, but usually out West to Oklahoma or Texas. And, of course, the fear of reprisal from the surviving Brooks clan always served as a compelling deterrent to a thorough investigation or exhaustive search by the apprehensive authorities.

So by 1892, twenty-eight years after the death of Willis and John Brooks, there were seven notches in Aunt Jenny Brooks' hickory stick. Only Sherm Williams had eluded the family.

But then, in June of that year, Junior Brooks, a part-time cowboy and full-time bootlegger now living in McKinney Texas, received a telegram from his ma in Alabama, informing him that they had finally located the single, remaining member of the Lawrence County Alabama Home Guard. Junior caught the next train east to Huntsville, Alabama.

The Hotel Monte Sano Dining Room

CHAPTER THIRTEEN

MR. DENISON DOESN'T HAVE MUCH for me to do on Saturday, so I'm helping out Oliver at his shoeshine stand in the lobby. It's pretty slow this morning, and I'm sitting in one of the customer chairs reading the *Hotel Monte Sano Breeze* and *The Democrat*, that, as usual, is filled with all kinds of editorials and letters about how social equality of the races is such a bad thing for both races, when who should show up but a cute, little, dark-complected girl with a bright twinkle in her big brown eyes.

"Are you Smokey?" she asks me.

"Yes, ma'am, I am, and who might you be?"

"I'm Sophie Franklin in Room Two-seventeen. I'm a friend of Jude's. He's told me about you. May I talk with you alone?"

"Sure, come with me."

So, even though I know I shouldn't ever be alone with a white girl, I lead her over to the dining room that's empty at this hour, since it's between breakfast and dinner time. "What can I do for you, Miss Franklin?" I ask her.

"Well, I was wondering what happened to Jude. We went riding the other day and came back a little late, and I haven't seen or heard from him since."

"Oh, he's okay. He's back to shoveling manure in the stable, and Mr. Rogers has forbid him to take you riding again."

"Can he do that?"

"Well, he done it," I tell her. "What about you?"

"I'm okay too, except my mama says I can't go riding with Jude again or even be alone with him. I don't think she and Mr. Rogers are being fair, but, anyway, that's the case."

"So what more is there to do?" I ask her.

"Well," she whispers, "I was wondering if you could give Jude a message for me?"

"I guess I could do that."

"Okay, tell him that if you and he are free tomorrow afternoon, I'm planning to take a walk to the Bottomless Well after church, at around two o'clock, on the trail at the end of the boardwalk."

"Him *and* me?"

"Well, Mama says I can't be alone with him, so maybe you could be our chaperone?"

"Chaperone, huh? I don't know about that," I tell her. "You know, don't you, that there's a rule around here that says hotel employees ain't supposed to git involved with hotel guests?"

"Who says anything about getting involved," she says with a sly smile. "I'm just asking for some company on a walk. There's not a rule against that is there?"

"I guess not, but I sure don't wanna see Jude git in any more trouble. Or you either, for that matter."

"I'll be waiting at the sign on the trailhead at two. Bye," she says and turns and sashays away.

Now, I could have, I should have, left it at that, and not said a word to Jude about my conversation with this little miss, but I didn't. I figured it would've come around and bit me in the ass one way or another, so I went ahead and told him what she said. You might of guessed how excited he was when I told him. He plum near jumped out of his suspenders.

"You'll come won't you, Smokey? So she doesn't get into any more trouble."

"I ain't so sure that's a good idea," I answer.

"Well, it's not for me. I sure as hell don't want you along, but if a guest asks you to do something, aren't you obliged to do it. They're always telling us how we have to please the guests, right?"

"I guess so, as long as Mr. Denison doesn't have something else for me to do."

"Well, it's Sunday, so it's not likely, and I suspect even Rogers will allow me one day of the week away from the manure pile."

"If you say so …"

Alum Spring

CHAPTER FOURTEEN

SO WE ALL MEET UP at the trailhead at two on Sunday. It's a hot, humid afternoon, so most reasonable people are napping in the shade someplace. But not us. Jude and his little miss are already mooning over each other when I get there. It looks like they've just come from church. There ain't a real church on Monte Sano yet — white or colored — but the white folks usually have a service on the hotel's porch or at someone's house. Jude's all dressed up in his Sunday best, with a clean white shirt and his hair all slicked back, and she's as pretty as a pitcher there in her long, white, lacy dress.

"Sure y'all wanna go for a walk in this heat?" I ask them. "Maybe we just as well go down to Cold Spring and sit in the shade."

"Naw," Jude says. "It's not that hot. We'll take our time and stop at Alum Spring to cool off on the way, and then we can climb the bluff at Abbey Rocks and cut back across the top of the mountain."

"Just as long as we're back by supper time," Little Miss says.

"No problem," Jude says.

So we take off down the trail. And even though we're in the shade most of the time, there ain't a lick of wind today, so it's rough going. Little Miss is surprised by the rockiness of the trail and complains that her fancy high-cut shoes are uncomfortable. So, just as we pass the Burton Mines, she takes them off and Jude offers to carry them for her. When, a little beyond the Broad and Maynard Mines, we finally get to Alum Spring, we're all tired and sweaty and thinking maybe hiking on such a sweltering day wasn't such a bright idea after all.

Major Scrimshaw and his men have landscaped the spring to look really fine. There's a nice little wood stave hut over the spring, and stone walkways around it, including a couple of wooden benches to enjoy the view. Since there's no one there except us, we go inside the hut to get out of the sun. We sit on the benches around the spring and Little Miss hikes up her skirts and puts her dusty feet in the pool. Jude and me, we ain't used to seeing girls' ankles cause they're always covered with skirts, so we stare like crazy. Little Miss notices.

"What?" she says. "Why are you staring at my feet? I know they're dirty, but ..."

"I'm sorry," Jude explains, "but Smokey and I don't have any sisters or mothers, so we're sort of ignorant about girls. You'll have to forgive us."

"Well, they're just feet, just like yours. So why don't you take your shoes off and join me?"

So we do. And I gotta admit it's real pleasant sitting there together with our sweaty feet in that little pool. Though I think it's a bit more pleasanter for Jude and Little Miss than it is for me, since they are soon playing footsy with each other, as if I'm not even there.

"So what's alum and what's it cure?" Little Miss asks, as she tickles Jude's toes with hers.

"Some sort of chemical," Jude says. "My daddy comes down here and gargles it when he gets a sore throat. Feels pretty good on sore feet, too, don't you think?"

"Mighty good. So Jude tells me you're from New York, just like me," she says to me. "What do you think of the South?"

"It's okay, I guess. It gits awful hot during the summer, in case you hadn't noticed, but it's better than freezing your tail off in the winter up north. And there're some real nice people down here. People always say that there's a lot of prejudice here, and they're right, but it's different from up north."

"How so?"

"Well, up north the prejudice is not so out in the open as it is here, but, as far as I can see, most white people up there hate colored people about as much as they do down here. Up north, the whites are nice enough to you on the street, but they still don't wanna be around you much. Down here they're pretty straight-forward. If they don't want you around, they just put up a sign that says: 'Whites Only.'"

"Doesn't that bother you?" she asks me.

"Yeah, sure it does. All these so-called Jim Crow laws are enough to drive any colored man crazy. Seems like you're always lookin' over your shoulder to keep from breakin' one rule or another. You'd think that as much as the white people down here depend on colored folks to pick their cotton, do their gardening, cook their food, clean their houses, and take care of their kids that they'd want to make life a little more easier for them."

"Why don't they, Jude?" Little Miss asks. "You're a Southerner."

"Oh, jeez," Jude answers. "That's a million dollar question. I don't know. White folks and colored folks have been working alongside each other every day down here ever since slavery times. We talk to each other. We joke around together. Like Smokey says, we depend on each other. But, you know, in the end, white people think colored people are inferior to them. That's the crux of the matter."

"But even if they think that," Little Miss says, "why do they have to treat them so bad?"

"The truth is," I tell her, "is that white people are afraid. In case you haven't noticed, we colored folks outnumber the white folks by a bunch down here. The white people are afraid of what might happen if they don't keep us down. They're afraid that if they don't keep us in our place, we'll all come out after them like that Railroad Bill fellow who's been killin' sheriffs and robbin' trains around here."

"Well, maybe so," Jude says, "but it doesn't really matter where you're at. Pretty much every race hates the other. Don't be fooled by what you see up here on Monte Sano. Up here's a little paradise, except for a few notable exceptions, where most everyone gets along with each other no matter what color they are."

"Like you and Smokey. You wouldn't see that in the North."

"Yeah, I guess not. Boys and girls in the South play with each other regardless of color up until the boys get out of knee pants and the girls out of pigtails, then something strange happens and they aren't that close any more. Except for Smokey and me, we sort of never got old yet, I guess."

"I think that's nice," Little Miss says.

"Well, it is most of the time," I says, "except when Jude acts like a jackass."

"Who you calling a jackass, you Yankee yahoo?"

"Boys, please. Put your shoes and socks back on, and let's get going before it gets dark. No telling what they'd do to us if we came back late again."

So we continue on in the heat, through dense groves of white oak, walnut, red oak, poplar, cherry, pecan, and sassafras. A bald eagle circles above and mosquitoes swarm below. When we reach South Drive at the southern end of the mountain, a red fox darts in front of us, and Little Miss screams and jumps on Jude like a duck on a June bug. Jude looks mighty surprised but also real pleased.

A little further on, Little Miss asks about how all the roads and trails got here. So Jude tells her, "The trails are mostly Indian trails, my daddy says, and the roads were either built by the coal miners to haul coal from the mines down into town, or the lumber companies to pull logs out on, or the early settlers to get from one place to the next. The hotel owners have added a few more around the hotel, but mostly they've improved existing ones."

So we continue on South Drive, an old settlers and logging road, past Sadler Spring, Glen Anna, Poplar Spring, Wildcat Glen, and Gordon Rock, a big limestone outcropping overlooking the hollow below, filled with more forests of hickory, dogwood, sycamore, and gum.

Finally, as the road begins to descend into the valley, we arrive at the Bottomless Well, just off the road to the left. What it is, is a big ol' round hole in the ground. They call it a pit cave. But me and Jude have been callin' it the Big Hole forever. The hole's about twenty feet across and goes straight down about two hundred feet through solid, gray, limestone walls all the way around it. It goes down as far as you can see and then turns into night, like a gaping mouth to hell.

There's no fence or anything around it, just a patch of scrub cedar growing out of the rocks, so we're careful not to get too close. Little Miss picks up a rock and tosses it down into the hole. After a while we hear an echo, like the rock hitting another rock or maybe water; it's hard to tell. We sit down on an outcropping nearby and stare into the hole.

"It doesn't sound like it's bottomless," Little Miss says.

"No, it's not" Jude says.

"How do you know?"

"Well, a couple of years ago, a man was leaning over to see if he could see the bottom and he lost his hat, and, lo and behold, a few days later it popped out of the Big Spring down in Huntsville."

"You're kidding?"

"No, really," Jude exclaims. "A guy over in Viduta didn't believe it either, so he took a live duck, put it in a basket, and lowered it into the well, and, sure enough, it came out quacking in a couple of days, none the worse for wear, right there in Big Spring."

"I don't believe you," Little Miss says. "He's lying, isn't he, Smokey?"

I have to laugh. Jude loves to lie. He's always telling folks there's a ghost on the mountain, and he likes to tell this story about the Big Hole goin' all the way down into Big Spring, and other nonsense like that. He don't mean no harm by it though; he just likes to spoof folks.

"Well, it's a good story, ain't it?"

"Yeah, but what's the truth?"

"The truth is," I tell her, "Jude is a lying sack of horse manure. Major Scrimshaw, the man who designed and tends all the gardens around the hotel, decided he was going down into the well three years ago. He rigged up a bucket connected to a steel cable and winch, like they use in the mines around here. But when it came time for his men to lower him down, he looked down the hole and decided better of it."

"Can you blame him?" Sophie says.

"Nah," I tell her, "I wouldn't go down there on a bet. But, back then, when ol' Scrimshaw chickened out, guess who they talked into being the first man to be lowered down."

"Who?"

"Why, a colored fellow, of course. A man named Jackson Lines, who still works for the Major, was either crazy enough or brave enough, dependin' on who you talk to, to be the first man to go down this here hole. He done it twice, and, on his second time down, he got sicker than a dog, cause that bucket, on that thin cable, was spinnin' around like a top. The Major finally did go down himself, just long enough to scratch his name on the well's wall, and then he came out of there as quick as a flash. No one's been down since."

"So what did they find down there?"

"Well, at a hundred and eighty feet, they found a big pile of rocks that folks, like you, had been tossin' down the hole forever. Scrimshaw said he heard some water dripping somewhere, but, as far as he could see, the water disappeared into the rocks and the so-called well was as dry as a bone. But he did measure the temperature while he was goin' down, and he said it was sixty-one degrees. Wanna jump down and cool off?"

"No, thanks!"

So we sit there and marvel at the site for some time, until Little Miss announces that we better head back. But before we do, she gets the bright idea of piling up some rocks on the rim of the pit near the road, so that when she comes back to show her mother and brother she'll be sure to find it. So we gather up some rocks and pile them up there next to the Big Hole. Now anyone coming down the road can easily see them.

We backtrack to Abbey Rocks, which is this high cliff with an outcropping of rock that forms this natural shelter about the size of the parlor of a house. Jude and Little Miss rest there in the shade, while I go looking around for arrowheads and a trap I remember setting around here someplace. I've found a few arrowheads up here before, but I don't see nothing today. But I do find a trap that's been triggered next to the dry, rocky streambed that goes through here. I put my boot on it to hold it still while I carefully raise the door, and, before I can get my hand out of the way, an ill-tempered raccoon flies out of there and rips into my hand. I holler and kick it away, but not before the little varmint takes a chunk about the size of a silver dollar out of my right wrist. I'm bleeding like an open spigot and it hurts like hell. So I go back to find Jude and Little Miss, who are still resting in the shade of

Abbey Rocks. Little Miss screams when she sees my bloody wrist and promptly lifts her skirts and rips off a piece of white cotton petticoat which she wraps around my bite. So with the bleeding slowed, we head back to the hotel. We climb up the dry creek bed to the top of the bluff. By the time we get there, we're all hot and dirty and sweaty and the sun is nearing the treetops over near Big Cove.

"How much further?" Little Miss gasps.

"No more than a mile down this road, East Drive," Jude tells her, pointing down the dirt road that goes across the plateau. "It meets up with Prospect Drive near Ella's Rock and then goes along the bluff to the hotel where it hits the end of the boardwalk in front of the hotel."

"Wanna race, since it's getting so late, and we're filthy anyway?" Little Miss asks. Jude and me look at her funny. We're no more used to seeing girls her age run races than we are seeing them lift their skirts to show their ankles.

"Just to see if you're any faster on foot than you are on horseback," Little Miss says.

"You're on," Jude says.

"Okay," I agree.

"Well, then, on three," she says, lifting up the hems of her dress and petticoats. "One, two, three ..."

And we're off. Little Miss quickly takes the lead, barefooted, holding her white skirts up around her tiny waist, pale legs and ribboned bloomers dashing through the woods. Jude is close behind her with one of her shoes in each hand. And me, bandaged and still bleeding a little, I'm just huffing and puffing to keep up.

I figure that since she starts out so strong that she'll tire soon, but she just keeps right on going. The top of the mountain is pretty flat along here, but there're still plenty of sharp rocks on the road. They don't seem to bother her though. But they bother me. About half way there, she and Jude are at least twenty yards ahead of me. And it looks like she's pulling away from Jude. Then, when we near the bluff and the boardwalk, I hear her scream. And it's not a little-girl scream either, like when she saw my raccoon bite. It's a scary, searing, full-throated howl of horror.

The Bluff Boardwalk

CHAPTER FIFTEEN

JUDE RUSHED TO SOPHIE'S SIDE and followed her teary gaze a few feet down the bluff to where a human body lay, twisted in a thick tangle of crawling vines, fresh blood oozing from its neck, wide eyes staring into the gathering dusk. "Take your shoes," he told her. "Run to the hotel and get Doctor Duffield. I believe he's dead, but Smokey and I will check. You get the doctor!"

Sophie wrapped her arms around Jude and cried into his shoulder. Jude hugged her back and whispered in her ear, "Go now. Get the doctor."

Smokey, winded and scared, found them there and looked over the bluff to see the body. As Sophie sprinted toward the hotel, he and Jude scooted down the bluff to the bleeding man. His arms and legs were weirdly askew and his neck was gushing blood from ear to ear. But his blank eyes told them what they needed to know. They were flat and lifeless.

"Who is it?" Smokey asked.

"It's Sherm, the man who works with me in the stable. Don't you recognize him?"

"Oh, yeah. He does look familiar, but awfully dead now."

"I think you're right."

"I ain't never seen so much blood in my whole life."

It didn't take Dr. Duffield long to confirm their diagnosis. But it did take a long while for them to dislodge the corpse from the greenbrier vines in which it was entangled. Soon Smokey's boss Mr. Denison was there and Jude's daddy and a lot of other curious folks. Once Jude and

The Hotel Monte Sano

Smokey and a couple of bellmen had finally disentangled poor Sherm and dragged him to the top of the bluff, a long discussion ensued on what exactly to do with him, whether to load him on a wagon and take him into town that night, or wait for the train to transport him there in the morning, or leave him somewhere on the mountain until the sheriff showed up to investigate.

It was finally decided that two bellmen would drag the body to an empty stall in the stable until the sheriff arrived. Waya, the fastest rider, would ride Shadow, the fastest horse, into town to rouse the sheriff. Meanwhile, in the overall panic and confusion of the moment, no one seemed to notice or care that Sophie, Jude, and Smokey had been first at the scene of the crime — together.

While the body was being carried away, Jude pulled Smokey over under the boardwalk in front of the hotel, away from the milling crowd. "I think we better go with the truth on this one," he told him. "Even if Sophie and I get in trouble for being together, it'll be too messy to try to lie our way out of it."

"I agree," Smokey said without hesitation, "but what about Sophie?"

"She's probably in her room by now."

"No, she's not," they heard her whisper from the boardwalk above. "Sophie!"

"But I better hurry up and get there before it gets dark."

"Did you hear what we were saying just now?" Jude asked her.

"Yeah, sounds good to me. Someone getting killed is a lot more important than our taking an innocent walk in the woods. Bye."

And, with that, she raced, skirts flying, down the boardwalk to the hotel's front door.

Jude washed up and changed out of his blood-stained clothes and waited in the stable, just a few stalls away from where the corpse lay lifeless and cold. He wondered who had slit Sherm's throat and why. The man seemed harmless enough. He wondered about death and how it came so quickly and senselessly. He had fretted about the death of his mother when he was younger, sometimes blaming himself for her demise. But when he told his daddy about these thoughts, his daddy had hugged him tight and whispered in his ear.

"Never, ever think that, son," he had said. "You did not cause your mother's passing. She died for no other reason than by the grace of God. And we have no reason to question that."

When the sheriff arrived later that evening, Smokey, at Mr. Denison's behest, began rounding up the people whom the sheriff wanted to question. When it was Jude's turn, Smokey ran into the stable breathlessly. "So far, he's talked to Mr. Denison, Doctor Duffield, and Sophie," he huffed. "Now it's your turn."

Sheriff Murphy, a burly man with a gray beard and serious blue eyes, was still dusty from his ride up the mountain. He had ensconced himself in a corner desk of the hotel's main parlor. He looked tired and spent when Jude sat himself down across from him in an uncomfortable oak chair.

"Tell me what you seen, son," the sheriff instructed.

So Jude told him everything that he could remember. When he was finished, the sheriff looked up from his notes and asked, "You know anybody who might have wanted this man dead?"

Jude hesitated. His boss A.D. Rogers immediately came to mind, since he and Sherm had argued so often, but he really didn't think Rogers would kill a man just because they didn't get along, and he didn't want to implicate him falsely or give the man a reason to dislike him any more than he already did.

"Well," he said, "Sherm had a sort of argument with one of the guests at a poker game in the stable a couple of nights ago. The man pulled a pistol on Sherm."

"Who was he?"

"A gambler, by the looks of him and by the way he played cards. I think he said his name was Comstock, but I can't remember his first name."

The sheriff made Jude go through the whole story of the poker game in detail, while the sheriff took notes in a little spiral notebook and asked a lot of questions. Finally, he asked, "What were you doing over by the bluff anyway?"

"I was returning from a walk," Jude told him.

"Who with?"

Jude told him the truth, as Smokey and Sophie and he had agreed earlier. Sheriff Murphy raised his eyebrows when Jude identified the unlikely threesome.

But, being unaware of Jude and Sophie's previous late outing, he simply listened and took more notes.

Even though Jude had told the truth to the sheriff, he somehow felt guilty and uneasy about what had happened. When, at a little past nine o'clock, the sheriff finally told him he was finished, Jude wondered back out on the porch of the hotel. No one was there at this hour, and it was quiet, except for the chirping of the tree frogs on the bluff and the cooing of a mourning dove in the rafters above. He wanted so much to stop and ask Sophie if she was okay before he went back to the stable, but he knew that it would only upset Sophie's mother and he didn't want to do that. Why, he wondered, did things have to be so complicated. But, as he stood there on the porch alone, hurting to see her, he realized how much he thought about this new girl from the North, and how much he cared for her, and how much he wanted to be with her. And he was more than a little puzzled and perplexed by what these strange new feelings were all about.

A Picnic on Monte Sano

The D. C. Monroe Orchestra

CHAPTER SIXTEEN

WHILE SHERM WILLIAMS' LIFE had ended, life at the Hotel Monte Sano had not. Jude found out from his father that Bradley Comstock, the poker-playing, pistol-packing guest on Memphis Row had checked out while the sheriff was questioning everyone and taken the last train down the mountain into Huntsville. And while no one had reproached Jude about his walk with Sophie on Sunday, he continued to shovel manure in the stable as usual. Smokey kept busy running urgent messages back and forth between Mr. Denison and Colonel O'Shaughnessy. And, as the rain and cool weather continued, Sophie stayed in her room, out of Jude's sight, but not out of his mind. He kept thinking about her and longing for her to reappear.

The murder and bad weather had put a temporary damper on hotel activities, but within a few days, the sun had returned, guests were playing croquet on the lawn again, men were back to cursing and smoking in the billiards room, women were having tea on the hotel's porch, and a few tipsy guests were laughing and ladling whiskey from a big bucket resting in the middle of the floor on the observation tower.

By Wednesday night, three nights after the killing, Jude heard the band playing again in the hotel's ballroom. And, if there was one thing Jude loved almost as much as horses, it was music, even if he couldn't dance a single step himself. Tonight's band sounded especially good, so Jude wandered over to the hotel, as he often did, to listen and peek in through an open window at the dancers.

He had heard so many good bands at the hotel. Professor Abbott's Orchestra was a local favorite. He also enjoyed Blind Tom, a former slave from nearby Athens, Alabama, who could play on the piano by ear any song the audience requested, from "Daisy Bell" to John Philip Sousa's "Reveille."

Tonight's group, according to its leader who was speaking into a megaphone, was called the D. C. Monroe Orchestra from Nashville, Tennessee, with musicians all the way from Cincinnati. There were six pieces: a coronet, a flugelhorn, a clarinet, a violin, a piano, and drums. The played a danceable mixture of the most popular songs of the day: "The Virginia Skedaddle," "Little Boy Blue," "Ta-Ra-Ra Boom-De-Ay!," "There Is a Tavern in the Town," "Oh My Darling Clementine," and many more.

When the orchestra took a break, a plump man with a megaphone mounted the stage and spoke to the fancy-clad crowd. "Ladies and gentlemen," he bellowed, "welcome to the beautiful Hotel Monte Sano. My name is L. C. Goodall, all the way from Olathe, Kansas, and I'm representing the American Jersey Cattle Club. Tonight it is my great honor to recognize the Monte Sano Dairy, its owners, and their fine Jersey cow, Signal's Lily Flagg, which, as of June first of this year, became the highest butter producing cow in the country." The crowd cheered and whistled. "And here to pass on the award-winning silver cup is none other than the owner of the previous record-holder, the illustrious Major W. J. Webster of Columbia, Tennessee."

As the crowd continued cheering, a smiling, mustached man hopped up onto the stage and was handed the megaphone by Mr. Goodall. "Thank you kindly. I am the owner of the previous winner of this beautiful silver cup," he said, holding up a rectangular chalice about the size of a loaf of fresh-baked bread. "Permit me, please, to read the inscriptions on it," he said, as he reached into his vest pocket and produced a pair of wire-rimmed spectacles which he carefully placed on his nose. "The first side reads 'Landseer's Fancy, 2876. Record, 936 pounds, 14 ¾ ounces, Columbia, Tennessee.' The second side reads 'Eurotisama, 29668. Record, 945 pounds, 9 ounces, Ipswich, Massachusetts.' The third side reads 'Bisson's Belle, 31144. Record, 1028 pounds, 15 5/8 ounces, Columbia, Tennessee.' That's my cow. And the fourth side, which is now blank, will be filled with Lily Flagg's new record and will read 'Signal's Lily Flagg, 31035. Record, 1047 pounds, ¾ ounces, Huntsville, Alabama.' Ladies and gentlemen, please welcome the owners of the Monte Sano Dairy and the new Jersey cow butter-producing champion of the world, Signal's Lily Flagg: General Samuel H. Moore, Captain Milton Humes, and Mr. William. E. Matthews."

The crowd cheered some more, as the three men pushed their way through the crowd to the stage. Then General Moore, a tall, taciturn young man who looked to Jude a little like the portraits he had seen of Abraham Lincoln, gave a long and flowery speech, thanking everyone from the dairy's manager, Mr. Matthews, to his mother, the cow, the United States of America, and God. "And finally," he announced, "in appreciation of this evening and all your support, I'm inviting y'all to the biggest ball the South has ever seen, at my home in downtown Huntsville on the twenty-first of next month. Please come and please enjoy the rest of the evening."

Then, finally, after all this business with a common cow, the band returned to the stage and soon the dance floor was filled. When they played "Shenandoah Waltz," the couples coupled and crowded onto the polished dance floor. And, as they gracefully circled the hall, there she was. Sophie, in a flowing white gown, was being held, as they waltzed by, by a tall, red-headed man who looked much older and taller than she. When her partner turned her to face the window where Jude stood, staring in, he saw that she was frowning. But when she saw Jude standing there, not more than ten feet away, Sophie's face lit up. But as much as he appreciated her smile, Jude was embarrassed and angry to be discovered peeking in like a banished child at a rich, lavish world he would never know. So he quickly turned away and stalked back across the lawn. Before he reached the road, he heard her shout, "Wait!" Jude, wait!"

And there she was dashing across the lawn toward him, like a little, white wisp of a ghost in the misty night. "Where're you going?" Sophie huffed when she had caught up to him and held his arm.

"Back to my lousy stall," he told her.

"Are you mad at me?"

"No," he lied. "Just tired … and sad, I guess."

"What are you sad about?"

"I don't know."

"Tell me."

He stared at her dark, brown eyes, as she tightened her grip on his arm. He really felt like crying at that moment, but he wasn't going to, no matter what.

"Jude?"

"Look," he finally said. "I haven't heard from you since Sunday when we found Sherm dead. I've been worried about you … that you might have got in trouble for taking a walk with me, that you might still be upset about finding Sherm's body. And then when I finally see you, you're dancing with … someone else."

"You're jealous, aren't you? That's your problem, isn't it? You're jealous because I was dancing with my new friend Clara's cousin, just some stupid boy who asked me to."

"I don't know," Jude said. "I've never … never had a real girlfriend before, so I'm not exactly sure how jealousy feels."

"Oh, is that what you think I am, your 'real girlfriend'?"

"Uh, I don't know. I like you a lot."

"Well, that doesn't make me your girlfriend," Sophie snapped, as she released his arm. "We hardly know each other."

"But …"

"And if I want to dance with somebody besides you, well, that's my business, isn't it?"

"Fine," Jude said, "dance with whoever you like. See if I care."

And with that, he turned his back to her and stalked back to his miserable stall in that familiar, but lonely corner of the stable.

The Monte Sano Railway

O'Brien's Button Hole Bridge on the Monte Sano Railway

CHAPTER SEVENTEEN

AND THEN IT STARTS RAINING AGAIN. The hotel is a strange and desolate place when it rains. It slows everything down, like a cold snap on molasses, except, of course, for the trains that continue to run at their usual speed and usual schedule, carrying guests who want to escape the hotel's lethargy and go to town to shop and look around. So the guests sleep late. The women who remain read on the porch and try to keep the children busy with stories and games. The men are bored and restless and take to the bar, the bowling alley, and the billiards room early on.

Mr. Denison is working on some numbers for Colonel O'Shaughnessy, so he tells me to take the rest of the day off. I go back to the stable. Mr. Rogers has gone into town to buy supplies and, I suspect, to relieve his boredom, maybe at Madam Mollie Teal's house. So a spirited poker game is going on out in a corner of the stable, as the rain pelts the tin roof.

"Smokey, how's your wrist?" Jude asks me when I come in drenched from the rain.

"Doc Duffield says I'm gonna live, if I don't get hydrophobia from the raccoon. He cauterized the bite with something called lunar caustic that hurt like hell. He said that should stop the infection from spreading if the raccoon's rabid."

"How will you know?"

"Well, if I start to gettin' depressed and bein' thirsty all the time, you better start diggin' my grave. So deal me in before it's too late."

So I pull up a chair and join the game. They're playin' penny-ante, as usual, so I throw a penny into the pot like everyone else, and Ivan deals us each a hand. I ain't got nothin', so I fold.

Waya asks for a couple of cards. "So who do you think did Sherm in?" he asks, to no one in particular.

"I'd bet on Rogers," Ivan says, as he tosses the cards to Waya. "Whatta you think, Smokey? You know about everything that goes on around here."

"I ain't sure," I says. "But I'm thinkin' maybe a man named Jay who wants O'Shaughnessy to sell the hotel," I says. "Whatta you think, Jude?"

"I don't know," he answers. "Maybe that man who pulled a pistol on him?"

"Well, could be. But whoever done it, I wish Rogers would hurry up and hire Sherm's replacement," Waya says. "I'm gettin' tired of workin' short-handed."

Waya wins the hand with three queens. He rakes in the pot to the pile of pennies in front of him, the biggest on the table. "Where'd you learn how to play poker?" Ivan asks him.

"From my granddaddy," Waya says, as Ivan deals the next hand. "He lived to be almost ninety and he could beat me at any card game we played up until the day he died."

"Where'd he learn from?"

"He fought with Andrew Jackson during the Creek War of 1813-1814, and the soldiers taught him — and were later sorry they did. By the time they'd fought the Battle of Horseshoe Bend, he'd won enough to buy his own little piece of land over by Turkey Town, where my daddy was born. But, in the end, it didn't much matter, cause he was forced to cede his land anyway a few years later. And then that two-faced, backstabbing Jackson forced the removal of the entire tribe in 1838, after all they'd done to help him defeat the Creek."

"How'd your family avoid that — the Trail of Tears?" Ivan asks.

"Granddaddy took his wife and four kids up on Borden Creek and hid them out in the woods, just laid low and hunted, trapped, and picked up odd jobs wherever he could to support them. He could grow anything too, so he had a big vegetable garden and some fruit trees. Daddy said they were poor, but the kids never knew it. And, in the end, even though it was tough, it was a far sight better than dying like the four thousand other Cherokee who were forced to march out west to Indian Territory."

As the rain continues to beat down, the card game drags on, and Waya keeps winning. Next to him, we watch a round pool of rainwater swell on the concrete floor from a leak in the roof above, as the rain blows against the stable in noisy, gusty sheets, on and on throughout the afternoon.

"What about you, Ivan? Where'd you learn to play?"

"From my daddy. Out on the farm, near Golightly, there wasn't much else to do at night. Once the chores and homework were done, all eight of us kids and daddy would play cards in front of the fireplace, while Mama knitted or read. What about you, Smokey?"

"Well, I guess I learned from a man named James up in New York City. James worked for Mr. Denison's family since way back when. And when Mr. Denison's parents died in a cholera outbreak in 1854, James raised Mr. Denison, since he was about twelve. James taught me about everything I know — how to operate a boiler, how to shine shoes, how to read a good book, and how to play cards too."

"What happened to him?"

"He died," I says, remembering the day Mr. Denison and I had stared in grief and disbelief at the telegram from New York, informing us of his death. "Of old age and influenza. Just last year."

"What about you, Jude?"

"I can't remember."

"What's wrong with you?" Ivan asks him.

"Nothing," Jude snaps back. "Just leave me alone and deal."

Ella's Rock

CHAPTER EIGHTEEN

DEAR DIARY,

MAMA IS ALWAYS TELLING ME that my sassiness will only get me in trouble. And, as much as I hate to admit it, she's right. The other night I had to open my big mouth and sass Jude about him being jealous of me for dancing with another boy. I should have been flattered that he likes me enough to be jealous. He even called me his girlfriend, I think. But instead I got angry with him for thinking he could tell me who I could dance with, even though he really didn't say that. I just sort of got carried away. I'm not sure why.

At any rate, when Jude took off back to the stable, I went back to the dance and found my new friend Clara Matthews, who's a niece of one of the owners of that silly cow they were all making a big fuss over. I told her what had happened with Jude. She told me not to worry, that boys were strange, and you could never tell what was going on with them. At least, she said, he seems to care about you.

Clara invited me to visit her in Huntsville and said she would be sure that I received an invitation to a big ball there that General Moore, one of the cow's owners, said he was planning. By that time, I was awfully tired and confused, so I told Clara, Mama and Jeremy that I was going to bed. Then I went back to our room and I cried for a while, and then I got so mad at myself that I couldn't figure out what to do.

I finally went to sleep, and then the next morning I went looking for Jude, but I couldn't find him. So today after breakfast I told Mama that I was going for a walk. I never did tell her that Jude, Smokey, and

I were together on Sunday when the man was killed, even though I admitted it to the sheriff. I think Mama suspected something, but she just didn't want to deal with it, and I know she didn't want to upset me any more than I already was.

So again I walked over to the stable, but Jude wasn't there. So I walked back to the hotel and found Smokey in the lobby at the shoeshine stand. I asked him if he knew where Jude was, but he didn't, so I asked him to give Jude a message for me.

"Tell him I'm sorry for the other night," I told him. "Tell him I was being crazy. Tell him I want to see him again. Tell him that I … Oh, just tell him to meet me at the south end of the boardwalk after supper tonight, at seven-thirty, if he can. Okay?"

"What happened?"

"Oh, Smokey, I've got such a big mouth sometimes. I'd be a lot better off if I'd just keep it shut."

"So y'all had an argument?"

"Sort of. It was mostly me, saying stupid things."

"No wonder he's been in such a bad mood lately. But, okay, I'll tell him you want to see him."

Then, at a little past seven-thirty, Jude, with a white flour sack slung over his shoulder, showed up at the end of the boardwalk. And I was so happy to see him that I threw myself at him and gave him a big kiss right on the mouth. And then he put his arms around me and kissed me right back. It was a good kiss too. Well, my first kiss, if truth be told.

While I apologized to him, Jude took me by the hand and led me down a path next to the bluff, not far from where we had found the dead man Sherm. "I wanna show you something," he said. After a few minutes, we came to a big outcropping of rock that jutted out over the steep bluff. From the rock there was a clear view of the sun setting on the wide valley below, shimmering Huntsville, and the glimmering Tennessee River fifteen miles to the south. It was the best view yet from the top of the mountain.

"Oh, it's so beautiful," I told him. "I wish it were mine."

Jude pointed to a carved word in the gray rock. It read "ELLA." My heart sank. Was this his way at getting back at me? Was Ella his real girlfriend, and now he was going to make *me* jealous by telling me how much he loved her?

"Who's Ella?" I asked him.

"Sit down and I'll tell you," he said, taking a quilt from his flour sack and spreading it across the top of the rock. "Many years ago, before the War Between the States, a famous man named Senator Claiborne Clay and his wife Virginia owned a summer home near here, on top of the bluff next to the Rison's house. It was burned, except for their barn, by the Union Army during the War Between the States, and Mrs. Clay sold all her property up here to Colonel O'Shaughnessy in 1886. But before all that, they enjoyed their summers here. One summer, Mrs. Clay's young cousin from Georgia came to visit her. And this cousin, whose name was Ella Hilliard, looked exactly like you. She had long black hair and dark brown eyes and was very pretty and full of life. That same summer a young man named James Donegan came to the mountain to visit his parents in their summer home. James' father owned most of the stores on the north side of the square in downtown Huntsville — Exchange Row they call it now — as well as a lot of land up here on the mountain.

"Well, one thing led to another, as they say, and the two became lovers. On one of their walks, they stopped here, and Ella gushed over the beauty of the spot and said that she wished she owned it, just like you just did. At which point, her lover James said, 'And so you shall. It's my father's, and I now give it to you, and tomorrow we will christen it in foaming champagne!' Which they did. And from that point forward it's been known as 'Ella's Rock'."

"What happened to them?"

"Well, it was true love, so they married, of course. But Ella died during the War. But twenty years after her death, her husband returned and carved the name you see next to you for all to remember."

"How romantic!"

"Yeah, but most everyone, except those of us who live up here, has forgotten that old tale, and there's no one left to vouch for its truth."

"But there's no doubt that there's her name carved right here on the rock," I said.

"That's true."

We peered out over the sun-splashed valley and held hands, until my curiosity could be contained no longer. "So what else do you have in that sack?" I asked him.

"A surprise."

"What kind of surprise?"

"Since Ella and James are all but forgotten, I've decided to re-christen this rock, even if me or my daddy doesn't own it," Jude said with a smile, as he pulled out a big green-glass bottle of champagne. "Compliments of Mr. Avery in the hotel's bar."

"Oh, my," was all I could think to say.

With that, Jude twisted the wire from the bottle's cork and then eased the cork out. It went flying with a pop over the bluff and the warm champagne bubbled out over my skirt, the quilt, and Ella's Rock. "I hereby re-christen this rock," he announced, "as Sophie's Rock. May it ever so remain!"

Then he threw his arms around me and kissed me. After the kiss, he produced two champagne flutes from his sack and filled them. There wasn't a lot left after the re-christening, but there was enough to make me feel warm, a little fuzzy, and truly in love.

Sophie Franklin
July 1, 1892

The Urn at the O'Shaughnessy Place

Lily Lake and the Foot Bridge

CHAPTER NINETEEN

I'VE BEEN RUNNING all over the mountain, rain or shine, for Mr. Denison and the sheriff ever since we found Sherm dead. From what I've overheard from Colonel O'Shaughnessy and his friend Jay, the deal to sell the hotel to the South Dakota investment group is heating up, especially now that there's been a murder at the hotel. The sheriff is all set up in a coat check room next to the ballroom and has been interviewing a bunch of people. I know who, because I'm the one who's been fetching them for him.

First, he talked to Dr. Duffield again, and then to Mr. Denison for a long time, and then to Jude and Sherm's boss Mr. Rogers, and even Colonel O'Shaughnessy. Now he asks me to go get him Major Scrimshaw, the man who's in charge of the grounds and the gardens around the hotel. Scrimshaw is a gruff, old man, with long curly brown hair that is usually covered by a wide-brimmed straw hat. He's really turned the lawn into a southern plant paradise, what with constantly blooming flowers, shrubs, and trees of one sort or another planted all over the place. I don't know them all, but I can now at least recognize the colorful beds of white hydrangea, red azaleas, and purple wisteria scattered around the grounds.

The old man could be almost anywhere, but I decide to first check the shed next to the kitchen in the back of the hotel where he keeps all his tools and equipment. He's not there, but one of his men tells me he's planting flowers over by the lily pond near the O'Shaughnessy Place. But, when I get to the pond, instead of Scrimshaw, I find this strange man, Will, who works for him, the man I'd seen sharpening his knife and bleeding into the creek and laughing like a loon over in McKay Hollow. This time he's bent over next to a wheelbarrow and violently hacking away with a rake at a bed of what looks to me like violets and honeysuckle. I watch, astonished at the viciousness of his chopping. When, gasping for breath, he seems to be done with his attack, I ask him, "You seen Major Scrimshaw?"

The man jerks around to face me, a scowl on his sweaty, red face. Then he reaches down to the ground where he was chopping and pulls up by its tail a bloody, four-foot long timber rattler. He holds it out at arms-length, like a thick, limp, brown rope, for me to see. "I hate these vermin! You want it, boy?" he asks in a deep backwoods Alabama drawl.

"Nope," I tell him. "Do you know where Major Scrimshaw is?"

"Who wants to know?"

"Sheriff Murphy wants to talk to him."

"The sheriff, huh?" the man says, as he drops the snake on the ground and spits a line of tobacco juice at my feet. "What, you the sheriff's nigger?"

"No, sir. I work for Mr. Denison, but I'm helpin' the sheriff find people he wants to talk to."

"'Bout what?"

"About the man that was killed here last Sunday."

Will stares at me with wild, squinting eyes, spits again, and snarls, "Tell the sheriff that Scrimshaw ain't here, but first take this empty wheelbarrow back to the barn."

"I don't have time," I tell him. "I've got to find Major Scrimshaw."

"You do what I tell you, boy!"

"See you later," I say and take off around the corner of the gazebo.

"Why, you lazy, good-for-nothin' coon," he hollers, as I run as fast and as far away as I can from this dumb, disgusting dog of a man.

Malinda Rowe's Grave

The Front Porch of the Hotel Monte Sano

CHAPTER TWENTY

DEAR DIARY,

I'M SITTING OUT HERE on the front porch, outside our room, in the early morning mist before anyone else is awake. And I'm shaking and scared, because a few minutes ago, when it was still dark, just before morning and all the birds started singing, a chilly wind swept through our room and woke me up. I looked around, and, in the corner, at the foot of Jeremy's cot stood a wispy figure in a long, white nightgown, staring down at me. I was so afraid, I didn't know what to do.

"What do you want?" I finally asked her.

"My husband and my two sons," she whispered.

"Who are you?"

"Malinda Rowe," she answered. "I used to live here many years ago."

"Oh, yes, I've heard about you."

"Is this my son?" she asked, looking down at Jeremy, whose arms and legs were slathered in calamine lotion to soothe the nasty sores that had opened up from the poison ivy he had tramped through while he was chasing a deer.

"No," I told her. "That's my brother Jeremy."

`"Oh, that's too bad. Have you seen my sons?"

"No," I said, "but I've seen your gravestone."

"I know. I used to teach pretty girls like you at my school not very far from that cemetery."

"I'm afraid your school is no longer standing."

"I know, but I'm thinking of starting another one. Would you like to come with me and attend it?" she asked, extending her hand and moving toward me.

"No," I gasped, and then I ran away from her, out here to the porch, leaving Mama and Jeremy still sleeping soundly in the silent room with Malinda Rowe's beckoning ghost.

I guess the Rowe Cemetery must have spooked me. But now everything seems normal again. The cooks must have arrived in the kitchen, because I can smell bacon and eggs cooking somewhere below. And I can hear the faint voices of people waking in their rooms downstairs. This is the best time of the day here in Alabama, before the sun fully rises and heats up the day, when there's usually a little breeze blowing and your dreams are fading fast and the birds are singing so loudly that you can scarcely sleep. Jude has been trying to teach me how to recognize the birds by their songs, but the only ones I recognize for sure are the cardinals, song sparrows, and mockingbirds, but I can identify several others by sight.

Jude and I have worked out a way to communicate, so we can see each other more often. There's a news stand and cigar bar right off the hotel's lobby, and Jude's friend Jim Robinson operates it. Jim carries all the local newspapers — *The Huntsville Weekly Democrat*, *The Evening Tribune*, *The Weekly Tribune*, *The Weekly Mercury*, *The Argus*, as well other national and regional newspapers, like *The Memphis Appeal*, *The Nashville Banner*, *The Atlanta Journal* and *The Atlanta Constitution* — not to mention a row of cigar boxes filled with a bunch of those smelly things. We simply leave a note with Jim or a verbal message, and Jude and I check in with him whenever we can. This way we can set up meeting times and places any time we like. But Jude is so busy at the stable now that Sherm is no longer there that I don't get to see him as often as I would like. I tried to talk Mama into letting me go riding with him again, but she won't hear of it. And when Mama arranged a carriage ride to Marion's View for us all — her, Jeremy, and me — Mr. Rogers made sure that Waya was driving the coach and not Jude. So mostly Jude and I take walks in the evening after supper. Mama trusts me to take walks by myself, but she won't let me go out alone after dark. That means that Jude and I usually have only an hour or so after supper when he gets off work before the sun goes down. Fortunately, Jude knows a lot of places on the mountain where we can get away from everyone and be alone: Earthquake Glen, Brigand's Den, Abbey Rocks, and, of course, Sophie's Rock.

Last night we walked to Rowe's Cemetery again, and we sat on a blanket on the ground at the base of a hickory tree, a few feet from Malinda Rowe's obelisk grave stone, and we talked. Jude is all excited about the Independence Day Celebration in Huntsville. He says that most of the hotel's guests go to it, riding down in the train, or the Tally Ho, or other carriages. Jude has to drive a carriage full of guests, and then there's a big parade, a picnic, and a baseball game. Jude plays a position called shortstop for the hotel's team that they call the Katydids.

He wants me to see him play, and we're trying to figure out a way to go to the parade and picnic together without Mama finding out.

Now the sun is shining through the leaves in the trees, the birds are singing, and I am missing Jude and looking forward to another day on Monte Sano.

Sophie Franklin
July 2, 1892

The First National Bank Building

CHAPTER TWENTY ONE

JUDE, SOPHIE, AND SMOKEY had agreed that they would try to meet on the steps of the big First National Bank building on the square in downtown Huntsville. The Independence Day parade was scheduled to start at noon, but none of them knew exactly when they would arrive, since they were all going separately.

Mr. Rogers, as it turned out, had assigned Jude to drive Mr. Denison and Sheriff Murphy down in one of the small carriages. The sheriff had been staying at the hotel for the last several days while he was investigating Sherm's death, but now apparently he wanted to return to town. Mr. Denison wanted to check on the Huntsville Hotel, see the parade, and coach the hotel's baseball team in its game against the Huntsville team later in the afternoon. Jude knew from Smokey that Mr. Denison had left his daddy in charge of the hotel while he was away, not that there would be that much to be in charge of, since most everyone was going to town for the day. But Jude knew that this would please his daddy, who didn't take much stock in cities or celebrations and would be perfectly content spending another quiet day on Monte Sano.

Sophie was taking the ten o'clock train down with her mother and brother. Even though it was Monday, the rail schedule had been expanded for the day to the Sunday schedule to accommodate the guests, with trains going up the mountain at nine in the morning, and one, four, and six o'clock in the afternoon, and down at ten in the morning, and in the afternoon at two, five, and ten. An extra train had been added to go up at eleven o'clock after the fireworks.

Mr. Denison gave Smokey the day off, so he was going to try to hitch a free ride on the back of the Tally Ho or hop on the end of the train on a slow curve when no one was watching, so he wouldn't have to pay for the "privilege" of sitting in the last car of the train with the smokers and any Negro servants who had been lucky enough to get the day off.

Jude had the carriage all ready to go by eight o'clock, but Smokey didn't come over to tell Mr. Rogers they were ready to go until after nine. While the Tally Ho took a few hours to make the trip down the mountain, a carriage was faster than the wagon. As long as his passengers didn't want to stop too often, they could make it down in a couple of hours. The carriage that Rogers had assigned Jude was one of the best, with a roomy, plush leather seat in back for his riders, and a wooden bench in front for him, all shaded from the sun with a black canvas top. Otherwise, it was open to the fresh morning air. The Monte Sano Turnpike had been built in 1859. It ran from the top of Monte Sano, near Cold Spring, to the Maple Hill Cemetery in Huntsville. Its surface had recently been refurbished and had been coated with a layer of fine crushed rock, so the ride was smooth and Ned's gait even and quiet enough that Jude could catch snatches of the conversation between his passengers behind him.

"I don't know," he heard Sheriff Murphy say. "I've talked to a lot folks on your staff. I didn't need the doctor to tell me that someone slit the man's throat with a very sharp instrument. That was obvious. But the question remains who and why."

"Any suspicions?" Mr. Denison asked.

"Well, apparently the murdered man and his boss Rogers didn't get along very well, but then again this Rogers fellow doesn't seem to get along very well with anyone."

"That's true. If he wasn't Colonel O'Shaughnessy's cousin, he would have been fired a long time ago, but I'm not sure his temper is foul enough to cause him to slit a man's throat."

"Me neither," the sheriff said. "I talked to the man, and he swears he was in the stable when Williams was killed, though everyone else who works there was at supper at the time."

"So anybody else?"

"Well, there's the man Bradley Comstock who pulled a pistol on Williams when he accused him of cheating at cards. He conveniently disappeared soon after the murder, and we haven't been able to track him down since. When he registered, he wrote down that he was from Louisville, so I've sent a telegram to the police there to see if they know anything about him. And I haven't heard back from them yet."

"Who else?"

"Well, I talked to Scrimshaw, since he has pretty much the run of the grounds, to see if he had seen or heard anything suspicious, but he didn't know anything either. I also talked to your chef, Connors, and he couldn't think of anyone who knew or cared about the man. And I've talked to everyone in the stable where he worked, and, aside from the general dislike of Rogers and this argument with Comstock, there doesn't seem to be anything there either."

"So where does that leave us?"

"Up the well-known creek, I'm afraid," the sheriff sighed. "I haven't questioned any of your guests, except the young Franklin girl who discovered the body, but that may be the next step. But the truth is, I don't have a clue to where to go next. You have any ideas, Mr. Denison? I know we've been over this before, but do you know of any employees or guests who might have had a reason to kill this man."

"No, not really. Sherm seemed to be an innocent enough fellow who seemed to get along with everyone, except Rogers, of course. And none of the guests have been a bit suspicious, except for this Comstock fellow."

"Tell me again what we know about this man Sherm?"

"Well," Mr. Denison said, "like I said before, the man's full name is Sherman Ralph Williams. His application says he has no next of kin and that he's from Moulton over in Lawrence County. He's fifty-five years old, fought briefly in the War Between the States, until he was injured early on, and was sent home, where he worked in a blacksmith shop up until 1864, when he upped and left Lawrence County and began working a bunch of odd jobs on farms, stables, and blacksmith shops around Alabama, Tennessee, and Georgia. This was his second season with us, and he hasn't caused us any trouble, as far as I know."

"Tell you the truth," Sheriff Murphy said, "I'm stymied. I wired the sheriff in Lawrence County, but he just wired back and said he couldn't find any of the man's family still around there — that's why we buried him here in Maple Hill.

"Trouble is it's been almost thirty years since he lived over there, and I guess people have already forgotten about him. The sheriff said he'd keep asking around and let me know if he found out any more about the man, but I haven't heard anything yet."

"Meanwhile, I just hope nothing else bad happens. My guests are spooked enough as it is, and if, God forbid, anybody else gets hurt, I might as well close up shop for the season."

"Well, barring any emergencies in the valley," Sheriff Murphy said, "I'll be back up here in a few days. After I hear from the police in Louisville or if I hear anything else from the sheriff in Moulton, I'll come back and keep questioning your staff and any guests who may have come in contact with the man."

The rest of the ride down the mountain was uneventful. The only two stops they made were at Fagan Spring to water the carriage occupants and, of course, Ned, and at the toll house to pay the twenty cents toll. There had been talk of the County taking over the road and eliminating the tolls, but since the mountain road was hard to maintain, and most people who owned cottages on the mountain could afford the toll, Colonel O'Shaughnessy's North Alabama Improvement Company continued to collect the fees. Soon they arrived at the sheriff's office on Church Street, where both men got out, and Mr. Denison told Jude to meet him for the game at the baseball field on the east side of town at three o'clock.

Jude drove the carriage over to the Penson and Pierce Livery Stable on Washington Street, cooled and watered Ned, and then ran to the square to meet Sophie and Smokey.

The square was crowded with men, women, and children of all ages, many dressed in red, white, and blue for the day's festivities. Jude pushed his way through the throng to the bank's pale limestone steps that were already packed with spectators waiting for the parade to arrive. Jude scanned the steps and finally sighted Smokey, one of the few Negroes there, up at the top, under the covered porch, in the shade right behind Sophie and her mother and brother. Jude waved. Smokey saw him and waved back and then pointed to Sophie in front of him and a step below. Jude maneuvered his way through the crowd, up the steps on the far side and around to Smokey, without Sophie seeing him.

"Now what?" Smokey whispered. "That's her mother and brother there with her."

"Beats me. This is as far as our plan went."

Smokey shrugged. They all waited there for several minutes looking up Jefferson Street in hopes of seeing the start of the parade. Sophie, dressed in a simple white cotton dress, never looked back, and Jude was growing more anxious by the minute. He didn't know what to do, but he so much wanted to draw her attention. And he was so close he could smell a faint hint of her now-familiar lilac perfume. So, finally in exasperation, he bent over and gently touched her waist. Maybe not as gently as he had intended, because she jumped and gave a little, surprised squeal. Everyone turned — Sophie to Jude and Smokey and the other Franklins to Sophie — everyone looking curiously at each other.

"Mama," Sophie finally said, "this is Jude Schrimsher and Smokey ... Smokey, what's your last name?"

"Woods," Smokey said.

"Smokey Woods," Sophie continued. "They work at the hotel."

"Well," Mrs. Franklin said, "pleased to meet you, I'm sure. And tell me, boys, what it is that you do at the hotel?"

Jude was struck dumb by Sophie's mama's beauty and insistent voice, so much like Sophie's that he was, for the moment, in a continuing state of, well, stupefied struck-dumbness.

"I work for Mr. Denison, the hotel manager," Smokey said.

"Jude ..." Sophie prompted.

"I ... I work for Mr. Rogers in the stable," Jude stammered.

Mrs. Franklin looked him over carefully and then asked him, "And do you, by any chance, accompany young women out beyond a reasonable hour on horseback excursions?"

"Well," Jude said, "not ordinarily, not on purpose."

"So it was an accident that you kept Sophie out past dark, making me sick with worry?"

"Yes, ma'am," Jude said. "I'm sorry. I meant no harm."

"Well … I guess no harm was done, but I'll thank you to show better judgment in the future, regarding me, and most importantly my only daughter and her well-being."

"Yes, ma'am," Jude said.

"So now, tell me about this town and why Sophie dragged Jeremy and me here to celebrate this Independence Day," Mrs. Franklin said.

"Okay," Jude said, embarrassed, sweating in anxiety, trying to remember some of the local history that he'd been taught in school and, when he couldn't, making stuff up and blathering on like some southern, pontificating politician who didn't know what the hell he was talking about or even why he was saying the stupid things that he was spouting. "Well, first off," he mumbled, "you're standing on the steps of one of Huntsville's earliest and most famous buildings. It was designed by George Steele, one of the town's best-known architects. He also designed the court house right across the street. Both were built in 1835, mostly by Steele's slaves, who did all the detail work of these and several other homes and buildings designed by Steele in and around town. These six columns next to you — I think they're called Ionic — were carved in Baltimore and floated down the Tennessee River to here on barges. Several banks have used the building over the years, but most people around here just call it the Marble Palace, even though it's made of white limestone mined on Monte Sano. There are rooms in there for the cashier and his family, and I've heard there're even cells in there to hold people who don't pay back their loans. But the thing I like best about it is not its architecture, which I think they call Greek Revival, but the fact that it sits right on top of a cliff, and, at the bottom of the cliff in back, is the Big Spring, which is pretty much the center of everything in Huntsville. I also like the back door of the building that opens into mid-air about fifty feet above the spring. I always imagine someone forgetting to lock that door, and an unsuspecting customer, thinking it was the water closet or something, deciding to open it and surprise …"

"Can we see the door?" Jeremy asked.

"Sure, after the parade, we'll go down to the spring for the picnic, and I'll show you."

"Jude," Sophie's mama said, "how is it you know so much about this bank and George Steele?"

"Well, I go to school here in Huntsville, and they pound this stuff into your head at an early age, whether you like it or not. One thing you can say about the people in Huntsville — they may not be the most sophisticated people in the world — but they're a bright, proud, and, for the most part, an educated lot."

"I'm impressed," Mrs. Franklin said.

"There's one thing about ol' George Steele they don't teach you in school though," Smokey whispered.

"What's that?"

"Well, everybody knows about it, especially colored folks. They just don't put it in the history books. Seems that when Steele died in 1855, he left a will that said a certain family of slaves that he owned — a twenty-three year-old mother named Bet and her four mulatto children — were to be freed, set up on a farm in a free state up north, and given enough money for them to live comfortably for the rest of their lives."

"How kind of him," Sophie said.

"Are you suggesting," Sophie's mother asked, "what I think you're suggesting?"

"What?" Sophie said.

"Yep," Smokey answered. "Everybody pretty much assumes who the daddy of those four little babies was."

"Oh," Sophie said. "Is that a true story, Jude?"

"I don't know. Of the only two people who know for sure, one is dead and the other is relaxing on a little farm up in Illinois."

"Look," Jeremy exclaimed, "here comes the parade!"

The parade's participants gathered at the Fairgrounds on the corner of West Clinton and Seminole Streets and proceeded northeast on West Clinton to Jefferson where they turned right, marched to the courthouse square, along Bank Row, then turned left on Eustis Avenue for one block, called Commercial Row, and then left onto Washington Street, Cheapside Row, then back over to Church, and on to the train depot where they dispersed. The bank building where the little group from the Hotel Monte Sano stood was on the square at the northwest corner of Jefferson and Eustis.

First, came two policemen on horseback, each with a flag flapping in the hot July breeze. One flag was the American stars and stripes, now with forty-four stars, and the other was the familiar Confederate stars and bars. Then came a waving, smiling Mayor Jere Murphy in his bunting-draped white carriage. Then there were several more official-looking people, all waving little American flags and beaming to the crowd. Jeremy jumped and squealed with delight when the twenty-strong Huntsville Coronet Band broke into Sousa's "The Washington Post" march on its turn onto Commercial Row.

A wagon full of cotton bales and thirteen pretty girls in white cotton dresses passed by next. It was drawn by four white horses harnessed in white. Each girl smiled and waved and held up a silver sign with the name of a cotton-producing state on it.

Various groups of men on horseback rode by, and the loud, ringing bell on the city's horse-drawn fire truck made Jeremy laugh and wave. The new Spring City Cycling Club passed, and a group of about fifty women in wide-brimmed, colorful hats walked by with two large posters that read: "Huntsville League of Women Suffrage" and "Women Bring All Voters Into the World — Let Women Vote."

"What do you think about that?" Jude asked Sophie.

"Absolutely," she answered. "They should be voting and the sooner the better!"

"Then what about Negroes, like during Reconstruction?" Jude asked.

"They still got the right to vote, according to the Constitution," Smokey said, "but not according to the redneck vigilante thugs who scare colored folks away from the polls whenever it's voting time. And in Florida and Mississippi they've already gone so far as to change their Constitutions to keep Negroes from voting. Lotta folks figure Alabama will be next."

Then there was a funny wagon from the Monte Sano Dairy. At the front was a small replica of a barn, with some limbs that Jude guessed were supposed to be trees, and lots of flowers and grass. But the best part was a little girl dressed like a milk maid, sitting on a stool, and actually milking a real-life cow.

"Is that that famous cow?" Jeremy asked.

"I don't know, could be," Jude answered. "But I doubt it. That cow's too valuable to be riding around in this heat on the back of a wagon."

"Where's this Monte Sano Dairy?" Sophie asked. "I've never seen it."

"Well, it ain't exactly on Monte Sano," Smokey said. "Actually, it's on the side of Chapman Mountain near Monte Sano. They've got lots of land over there and a big house called Gladstone Place, and over forty head of these Jersey cows. They make enough milk, butter, and cottage cheese to supply most of Huntsville year round, including the hotel."

The Huntsville Gun Club marched by in gray Confederate uniforms with their rifles on their shoulders. "Ask those guys about Negro voting rights," Smokey said. "You should of seen 'em last August. They came up to the hotel and had a big ol' shoot and barbecue that lasted all day. But instead of clay pigeons they were shooting at real birds. All told they shot almost five-hundred pigeons and about a thousand swallows. Then they had a big barbecue and these guys drank so much whiskey that by the end of the day they were fallin' down drunk all over the lawn, and most of 'em couldn't even make it back down into town until the next morning."

Then a group of about twenty women dressed in long white dresses marched by with signs that read "The Women's Christian Temperance Union" and "For God and Home and Native Land." Jude said, "Carrie Nation came through here a few months back and slung her hatchet through the mirrors in the Dewdrop Saloon. Men were running out of there with mugs of beer in their hands and fear in their hearts, let me tell you."

Jeremy pointed and laughed at Willie Strange riding on his high, big wheel bicycle, wearing a shallow crown derby; red, white, and blue sleeve garters; and three-quarter length trousers.

Near the end of the parade an elegant, long black carriage appeared. Shaped like a quarter moon, it swooped down in the middle and up in the back and front, where a uniformed driver sat and held the reins of two big black stallion horses. And in the carriage were half a dozen of the most glamorous women Jude had ever seen, all dressed in white, lacy, long dresses, and satin, feathered hats, and holding elegant, delicate, pink parasols. Unlike ordinary women they wore bright red lipstick and rosy rouge and dark eye liner and shadow.

"What in the world?" Sophie said.

"Mollie Teal and her gals doin' a little advertisin'," an ogling man in front of them remarked.

"Who's Mollie Teal?" Jeremy asked.

No one answered, but there was a bit of nervous laughter among the men.

"Who?" Sophie insisted.

"Uh," Jude said, "if you must know, she's our local madam."

"Madam?"

"Yeah, you know … like …"

"That's okay, Jude," Sophie's mama interrupted. "I'll explain it to her later."

"Madam?" Jeremy said.

"Be quiet, Jeremy," Mrs. Franklin said. "Here comes another band."

And what a band it was. Festooned in tailored maroon and white uniforms, at least thirty strong, they high-stepped to the corner and blasted out the "Mardi Gras March." The crowd applauded and shouted for more, but the band marched on and the parade was over.

"Who were they?" Sophie asked.

"The State Normal and Industrial School band," Jude said.

"They were marvelous!"

"Why'd they put them last?" Jeremy asked. "Cause they're colored?"

"No," Smokey said, "cause they wanted to make sure people stayed till the end."

There were then speeches by local officials on the courthouse steps. Jude was genuinely embarrassed by the racist diatribe of a little fat man who was running for governor. "I vow, that if elected," the red-faced candidate exhorted, "we'll not spend one dollar for nigger education, because education unfits the nigger …" So Jude was glad and relieved when Mrs. Franklin said she was hungry and asked Smokey and him to show her, Sophie, and Jeremy where the picnic was being held. Jude led the way down Fountain Row next to the bank to the Big Spring where the fresh water flowed directly from the base of the bluff into a semi-circular basin, over a natural dam, and then into a narrow, manmade canal. Next to the pool was a waterworks building which housed a series of pumps that pushed the fresh spring water up to Echols Hill where a new sixty feet high reservoir stored sixty-thousand gallons of water to be dispersed throughout the city in lead pipes and, of course, up the hill to the Hotel Monte Sano.

"Look, Jeremy" Jude said. "There's the door I told you about."

"What did you learn in school about this spring?" Mrs. Franklin asked, as they walked across the footbridge next to the water works.

"Well, let me see what I can remember. It's the reason the town is here. A man named John Hunt brought his family here from Tennessee in 1805 and other families followed. A story you might like, Jeremy, is how these early settlers dealt with all the rattlesnakes that they found living in the crevices of the cliff."

"How?" Jeremy wanted to know. "Did they shoot them?"

"Nope, they hollowed out some canes, filled the canes with gunpowder, shoved them in the snake holes, and then lit them. Those snakes, the ones that weren't blown to bits, cleared out fast."

"What about Indians back then?" Jeremy asked.

"Yep, lots of 'em. The Cherokee and Chickasaw Indians hunted deer, bear, ducks, wild turkeys, and fish here — until the white men ran them off — but that's another story.

"The water from the spring is supposed to be some of the coldest spring water in the country, around sixty degrees. And it flows at the rate of about twenty-four million gallons a day, if I remember right, enough to power the pumps, supply the entire town, and to fill the

Indian Creek canal to float cotton boats all the way down to the Tennessee River."

"Who owns it?" Jeremy asked.

"Well, the city owns it now," Jude told him, "but it was originally owned by a man named Doctor Thomas Fearn who built a cistern up on the hill. From there he pumped the water in wooden cedar pipes to houses all over town. It was the second public water works in the country. He later deeded the spring to the city in exchange for free water for his family and his heirs."

"What was the first one?" Jeremy wanted to know.

"The first what?"

"The first water works. If the second one was here, where was the first one?"

"I can't remember," Jude answered. "Maybe Philadelphia."

West of the spring and waterworks and adjacent to the canal was a wooded park, now filling up with hungry people who were moving toward the long trenches of red hot coals where whole sheep, pigs, and calves were being roasted. Colored cooks turned and basted them with butter, bacon juice, red pepper, salt, and garlic. The aroma was tantalizing. Also smoking over the coals were big, black, iron wash pots filled with beef stew, Irish stew, and jambalaya. Five-gallon coffee pots steamed alongside. Tin tubs of pickles, potato salad, slaw, and relish rested on long lines of wooden tables. An old man unloaded watermelons from a rundown wagon, boys churned ice cream freezers in the shade, and women set out on open wagons cakes and cookies of all kinds. The picnic cost twenty-five cents a person for all you could eat.

Jude spotted Cook Cazzy's daughter Eliza Kendricks, his former wet nurse and the mother of the young botanist Ella who Smokey had courted last summer. She was slicing off thick slices of ham onto to a tin platter from a red pig still roasting on a large spit over the hot coals. She was sweating and flushed; but when she saw Jude, she handed the platter to the woman next to her and rushed to him, engulfing him her stained apron and strong arms. She was a tall, stout woman, the color of milk chocolate, who smelled of smoke, supper, and soil, and Jude hugged her and held her tight. She was the closest thing he had to a mother and he was always glad to see her.

To supplement his farming income, Jude's daddy worked in the coal mines on Monte Sano and also cut stone and did stonework around the mountain. While he was constructing a fence at Colonel Fearn's home on Monte Sano, he was assisted by the Widow Fearn's gardener, Leonard Kendricks, who was married to Eliza, who was the Fearn family's cook. Just a few months before Jude was born, Eliza had a baby girl named Ella. When Jude's mother died, there was no one else on Monte Sano who was nursing, only Eliza. And even though some of her family had frowned on it, she had volunteered to feed the little white baby, and Jude's daddy had gladly accepted.

Eliza told Jude about her new job as a cook for the John Matthews family over on Eustis Avenue, and Jude told her about Sophie and his summer at the Hotel Monte Sano.

"I swear," she laughed, "you's growin' up into a man, already. Why it seems like only yesterday you was just a little tike, tuggin' at my teat."

"Shush, Eliza, you say that every time you see me. You're embarrassing me."

"Don't you shush me, Jude Schrimsher, you ain't a man yet. And even if you was, ain't nothin' to be embarrassed about and you know it."

"I know," Jude laughed and hugged her again. "I love you, Eliza. I'm proud that you're my milk-mother."

Smokey staked out a big rock in the shade of an oak tree near the spring while the others filled their plates. And while Smokey got in the colored line, they sat on the rock and ate.

"Everything's so delicious," Mrs. Franklin said. "I've really become fond of southern cooking, I'm afraid. If we don't go home pretty soon, I'm going to have to let out all my dresses."

"When are we gonna go home?" Jeremy whined.

"I'm not sure," Sophie's mother answered. "We had planned to stay through most of August and return in time for you and Sophie to start school after Labor Day, but I received a letter from your father on Friday saying that he was missing us a lot and was concerned about our safety after the death of that man at the hotel. He wants us to come home sooner."

"Mama …," Sophie moaned. "Please, no, we just got here."

"I wanna go home," Jeremy groaned.

"Well, we'll see. Right now, you take these dirty dishes over there to that washtub where those ladies are cleaning up."

"Yes, ma'am," Jeremy sighed.

"Mama, please …," Sophie continued.

"We'll talk about it later," her mother said firmly.

Jude had not thought about Sophie leaving. He knew, of course, that she wasn't going to stay forever, but, up until now, her return home had seemed so far away. He was having a hard time imagining a world without her. Since they had established their little communication route via Jim Robinson in the news stand, they were seeing each other every day. Now her mother was threatening to end all that. And there wasn't a damn thing he could do about it. So they all sat there on the rock together quietly, each contemplating what this new pronouncement meant. Then they heard the splash and the shout from the spring near the base of the cliff.

"Jeremy!" Mrs. Franklin shouted, as she looked around and realized who was missing.

They all rushed to the spring. Jude got there first and jumped into the pool to pull a soaked Jeremy from the cold water. He wasn't in any real danger, since the pool was shallow enough for him to stand on the bottom with his head just above water, but he didn't know that, so he splashed around like a drowning man until Jude dragged him out. The dousing had scared him and he was crying and shivering even in the horrid heat. Someone produced a towel and he was soon whimpering into the shoulder of his relieved mother. After she had dried him off and calmed him down, Mrs. Franklin, looking tired and depleted, said she thought she had better take him back to the hotel on the next train. "I think we've had enough excitement for one day," she sighed.

"Can I stay to see the baseball game?" Sophie asked.

"Oh, honey, I don't know …"

"Please …"

"How will you get back?"

"On the first train after the game. I still have my return ticket."

As Jeremy squirmed, Sophie's mother contemplated.

"Jude," Mrs. Franklin finally said, "be honest with me now. Is it appropriate for a young lady to attend this baseball game by herself?"

"Sure. I'll be there, and Smokey'll be there, and Mr. Denison, he's our coach, he'll be there, and there'll be players' mothers and sisters and all kinds of folks."

"Well, it's those 'all kinds of folks' that I'm concerned about."

"I'll take care of her," Jude assured her.

Mrs. Franklin stared hard at Jude, and they all knew what she was thinking. Should she really trust this boy to take care of her daughter — the boy who had kept her daughter out late when they had first gone riding?

"Have her home before dark. She can watch the fireworks from the hotel's porch."

"Yes, ma'am."

With that, Mrs. Franklin dragged the sopping Jeremy off toward the train station a few blocks away.

Jude and Sophie stood beaming at each other. And Smokey leaned in very close to Ella Kendricks, who was drying dishes near the steaming washtub next to the canal, put his arm around her waist, and kissed her on her round, brown cheek.

The Huntsville Greys

CHAPTER TWENTY TWO

JUDE, STILL DAMP FROM HIS DIP in the spring, walked over to the wagon where the old colored man sliced him and Sophie two thick slices of red, juicy watermelon. They stood near the spring and ate the sweet melon, spitting the seeds onto the ground next to the pool. "I guess we better head on out to the ballpark," Jude told Sophie, as the pink juice ran down his chin. "You ever seen a baseball game before?"

"No, but I'm looking forward to it."

Jude tried to explain the game to her, as they rode the horse-drawn streetcar out Randolph Street to the ballpark. It was located between East Clinton and East Holmes, near the houses that were being built for the workers at the new Dallas Mill that was scheduled to open in November. Jude had read in the *Mercury* that the mill was supposed to have twenty-five thousand spindles and seven-hundred and fifty looms broad enough to weave the widest cotton sheeting made in America.

But the more Jude told her about baseball, the more confused Sophie became. She just wasn't catching on to the game very fast. "So what happens when you get three outs?" she asked him.

"The other team gets to bat."

"You mean they try to hit the ball at the other team?"

"Something like that," Jude laughed.

"Maybe Smokey can explain it to me while you're playing," she suggested.

"Well, I'm afraid not. Smokey'll be standing with the colored folks out in the outfield, and you'll be sitting in the stands with the mothers and sisters and girlfriends."

"That's not fair."

"I know, but that's the way it is."

"Why?" Sophie asked. "I thought the War changed all that."

"It did for a while, I guess, but then the white folks took over again and passed all these separate but equal laws — some call them Jim Crow — to keep the races apart."

"If the colored people have to stand in the outfield and we white folks get to sit here on the bleachers, that does sound separate, but not very equal. What if I was to go out and stand with Smokey and all the other colored folks?"

"You can't."

"But what if I did?"

"There would be trouble, and I promised your mama that I'd keep you out of trouble."

"Okay, but I still don't think it's fair."

The ballpark wasn't much, just a big green, grassy field with a red clay infield and a short row of wooden bleachers just off the first and third base lines. Several men pushed bunting-decorated wooden carts through the milling crowd, selling hot sausages, roasted peanuts, popcorn, Schillinger and Birmingham beer, root beer, and Dr. Pepper.

Jude took Sophie to the stands to introduce her to John Bakee's sister Lauren who was about Sophie's age. John washed dishes in the hotel kitchen and played third base for the Katydids, the hotel's team. But before he could locate Lauren, Sophie spotted Clara, the town girl she had met at the Lily Flagg reception at the hotel. Sophie rushed to her, and Jude followed. "What are you doing here?" Sophie asked her.

"That's my cousin John over there with the Huntsville team. He plays second base for them," Clara said, as she pointed to a group of young men in white flannel uniforms with "Huntsville" emblazoned in red across the front of their jerseys. "You remember him, don't you? I made you dance with him at the hotel."

"Oh, yeah," Sophie said, as she watched Jude blanch.

"And this must be Jude," Clara said.

"Yes," Sophie answered. "I'm sorry. Clara, this is Jude Schrimsher. And, Jude, this is Clara Matthews, the girl I told you about."

"Pleased to meet you."

"Pleased to meet *you*," Clara smiled.

"How's this Huntsville team doing this year? I've heard they're pretty good," Jude said to Clara.

"Oh, yeah. The Greys are doing great. That's their manager, W.W. Newman, over there. And they've got a new battery, Ebrenz and Hutchens. With them, we've already beat the Memphis Chickasaws, the Nashville Athletics, the Louisville Mutuals, and even the Cincinnati Shamrocks. So you're gonna have your hands full."

"Where are your uniforms?" Sophie asked.

"Oh, they should be over in that barn beyond right field. They were supposed to have come down from the hotel by train this morning. I guess I better go over there and get into one of 'em. Clara sounds like she knows the game, so she'll explain everything. I'll see you after the game." He kissed her and ran off to find his uniform and his teammates.

It was true that they didn't have much of a chance against the more experienced Huntsville team. Because Mr. Denison was trying to manage a hotel and all his players were working various schedules there, they didn't have much time to practice, and, when they did, there was never a complete team. The ball field that Major Scrimshaw had fashioned for them on Monte Sano was no more than a mowed field with three flour bags filled with sand for bases and a flattened lard can for home plate. But what they lacked in practice and equipment they made up for in enthusiasm and determination. So Ivan Demensher, the older boy who worked with Jude in the stable, kept them in the game with his sizzling fastball and sweeping curve — until he got tired in the seventh inning and the Huntsville bats came alive. Bob Girard, who worked for Jude's daddy as a bellboy, came in to relieve Ivan in the bottom of the eighth with one out and the Katydids trailing, 3-1. He got Huntsville's big center fielder Richard Pettybaum to ground into a double-play to end the inning.

Jude led off in the ninth and lined a single down the third base line. As he took his lead off first base, he eyed the Greys' tall, red-headed second baseman, John Matthews, the boy who had danced with Sophie at the hotel. Morris Dobbins, the Katydid's pudgy, right-handed first baseman was at bat. Jude had been studying Huntsville's pitcher Eddie Ebrenz all afternoon. He was sure he could steal on him, but Mr. Denison had not yet given him the sign to do so.

Ebrenz's first pitch to Dobbins was a fastball down the middle, but Dobbins didn't swing. His second pitch was another fastball that almost took Dobbins' head off, but he ducked just in time. Jude figured Ebrenz would try to tempt Dobbins on his next pitch with a curve out of the strike zone. He took an extra lead-off step, watched Ebrenz rest in his stretch, then at the split second that he committed, Jude took off for second. He heard the ball hit the second baseman's mitt a step or two before he arrived, so he raised his cleats and went in high and hard. He heard the second baseman's pants rip as his cleats slid through them, and then he saw the ball dribble off into the dirt as the second baseman flipped head over heels behind the base, landing hard and hasty on the back end of his butt.

"Safe," the umpire shouted.

The second baseman got up, dirty but unhurt, except for his pride and his torn trousers, and glared at Jude. Mr. Denison, in the coach's box, shrugged, smirked, and shook his head. Unfortunately, that was as far as Jude got. Nobody could bring him in, so that's how the game ended.

By the time Jude had changed into his street clothes, Clara was gone and Sophie was standing by herself next to the stands. He ran to her, and they went looking for Smokey, but he was already walking away with Jude's milk-sister Ella Kendricks. By then, it was almost six o'clock, so they still had a couple of hours before sundown.

"So why did you spike that boy?" Sophie asked him.

"I only got his pant leg," Jude said. "If I had wanted to spike him, I would have."

"Clara said you did it on purpose."

"She's right," Jude admitted. "I did do it on purpose, but not because I was jealous of him. I did it because we were down by two runs and we needed someone in scoring position, and the ball got there before me, so I had to try to make him drop it. It's just baseball."

"Are you sure?" Sophie asked.

"Trust me on this one. There would have been a fight if I had done anything wrong."

"Well, okay, if you say so," Sophie said. "What do we do now?"

"Well, we can either walk over to Clinton Street and you can catch the next train up the mountain, or we can walk a few blocks to the stable and take the carriage back. Mr. Denison said he was going back on the train and I don't see Smokey, so I guess it would be just you and me."

"If we take the carriage, will we get back before dark?"

"If we hurry."

"Okay, let's go."

"What about your mama's rule that we're not supposed to be alone with each other?"

"It's a little late to worry about that, don't you think?"

"I guess."

So they walked back to the Penson and Pierce Stable and hitched Ned up to the carriage and started up the mountain. At first, Sophie sat in back on the soft leather bench, and Jude sat in front on the driver's buckboard. But Sophie didn't like it back there all by herself, so she hitched up her skirts and crawled over the buckboard to sit next to Jude. "This seat's harder up here," she said, as she snuggled up next to him, "but it's not as lonely."

After they had stopped to pay the toll, Jude asked her, "So do you think your mama's serious about y'all going back home soon?"

"I don't know. If Papa wants us to come home and Jeremy wants to go home, I may be outvoted."

"What could change her mind?"

"Well, I guess if they caught the murderer, it would make Papa not so worried about our safety, but I really think something else is going on here too."

"What?"

"I think maybe when Mama saw us together today, she might have started suspecting that we are a little closer than she would like."

"You think?"

"I'm not sure. I just have this sneaking suspicion. Mama can read me like a book."

"And …?"

"And what?" Sophie asked.

"And what's the story that she's reading?"

"Wouldn't you like to know."

They stopped at Fagan Spring to give Ned a drink. Sophie rested her head on Jude's shoulder, and Jude put his arms around her. "I don't want you to go," he whispered. She looked up at him, and he kissed her.

When Ned had drunk his fill and they were heading up the mountain again, Sophie said, "Don't worry. I'll talk to Mama, and we'll figure something out. Do you know if the sheriff has any idea who killed the man?"

"No, he doesn't have a clue. He was talking to Mr. Denison on the way to town this morning, and he hasn't found out much of anything."

"So the murderer's still out here somewhere?"

"I guess, or maybe he took off. Who knows?"

"Maybe we should help the sheriff out," Sophie said.

"Whatta you mean?"

"Maybe you, me, and Smokey — since he seems to know everything that goes on around the hotel — maybe we should mount our own investigation. See if we can find the murderer."

"You're kidding?"

"No," Sophie said. "What do we have to lose? If we don't find him, all we've done is wasted some time, but, if we do find him, maybe we buy a little time and maybe I'll get to stay till the end of summer."

"What about these suspicions that you have that your mama thinks we're getting too cozy? And what about your papa being lonely by himself back in Schenectady? And Jeremy wanting to go home?"

"Let me worry about all that. Down deep Mama's a sap and appreciates a good love story just as much as the next guy, especially when it makes her only daughter deliriously happy. Papa's not really lonely. He's just saying that to be nice. He's gonna spend all his time at the plant anyway, whether we're there or not. I really do miss him, but

I'd miss him just about as much if I was at home. And, as far as Jeremy goes, that's easy. All I have to do is bribe him with candy. He'd jump off the top of the bluff if I told him there were sweets at the bottom."

"A love story, huh?"

"Just shut up and drive … cause if we don't get back by dark, it'll be the end of the story."

Dallas Street

CHAPTER TWENTY THREE

I WAS REALLY STUCK on Ella Kendricks, Cook Cazzy's granddaughter, last summer. She's very pretty and very smart, and the fact that she's Jude's milk-sister makes her that much more interesting to me, for some strange reason. She claimed last winter that she had a new boyfriend in Huntsville, and she didn't want to see me anymore. But when I see her at the picnic on the Fourth of July, she seems glad to see me.

"So what's the deal with your new boyfriend?" I ask her while she's drying dishes in Big Spring Park.

"He's an old boyfriend now," she informs me.

"What happened?"

"It's a long story."

So after the baseball game I walk her home to her house on Dallas Street. Her mother, Eliza, and her father who works as a gardener aren't at home yet. So we sit on the front porch swing behind the jessamine so no one can see us from the street, and we smooch, just like old times, and talk about life.

"I'll be honest with you," she says, between kisses, "it ain't easy havin' you up there on the mountain all summer and only bein' able to see you once a week."

"Ain't nothin' I can do about that."

"I know, but I git lonely sometimes."

"Me, too."

We're quiet for a while. A bumblebee buzzes around the jessamine, a mockingbird scolds us from a magnolia tree in the front yard, and a dog barks somewhere over on Holmes Street.

"Do you ever miss your parents?" she asks, snuggling up next to me. "It must be hard not havin' 'em. I cain't imagine."

"I ain't never known anything different, so I don't know. I guess it would be nice to have 'em around. A lot of the time, it does seem like there's somethin' missin', especially now that James is gone. But, then again, they'd probably be tellin' me what to do all the time. Leastwise, the way it is, I don't gotta worry about pleasin' nobody — except Mr. Denison — but he pretty much lets me do what I want as long as I do my job."

"But what happens when you're all grown up? You gonna be runnin' errands for Mr. Denison all your life?"

"No," I tell her. "I'm thinkin' about goin' back to New York City, or someplace up north, and gittin' away from all this separation mess they got goin' on around down here. Let me read you this article I cut out of the *Mercury* the other day. I been carryin' it around for a while now just to remind myself why I can't stay here forever."

I pull the wrinkled piece of newsprint from my back pocket and read it to her. "The headline says 'Another Negro Hung' and then it goes on like this: 'The telegrams last night contained the familiar story of another outrage on the person of a young white woman at Woodbury, Tennessee. The young Negro was captured near the scene and ere this one has danced the round dance at a neck-tie party'."

We sit there quietly. I think to myself that maybe I've said too much. We all know this stuff happens, but most of the time we don't talk about it. It's just too sad and dreadful, and too awful to face. Instead, we just let the anger simmer up inside of us. Someday, I think, it's all gonna boil over.

"Why is it," Ella says, "that these white men can gawk and stare and make rude remarks, and worse, to us colored girls and no one bats an eye, but when a Negro man even looks cross-eyed at a white woman, he gits strung up?"

"Don't ask me, I ain't made the rules. I read another article in a colored newspaper out of Memphis called *The Free Speech*. The woman that wrote the article, name of Ida B. Wells, I think, said that over a hundred Negroes had been lynched in the South just this past year."

146

"I know, seems like it's gittin' worse all the time too," Ella says. "I was helpin' mama out at her new job over at the Matthews and I overheard Mrs. Matthews and this other white woman talkin' bout all the colored men that's been gittin' strung up. Mrs. Matthews, she told this other woman it was because it's too big an ordeal for a self-respecting white woman to go to court and accuse a Negro ravisher and then withstand a public cross-examination. She said it was intolerable. No woman will do it. And, besides, the courts are uncertain. Lynching, she says, was the only remedy."

"I heard the President of the State Normal and Industrial School, William Hooper Councill, give a speech awhile back," I tell her. "He offered to make a contract with the white race that if a colored man broke the seventh commandment with a white woman, the Negroes would see that he was hanged, but if a white man broke the same commandment with a colored woman, then the white man would be punished according to the law."

"Ain't never gonna happen," Ella sighs.

"I know. That's why I'm headin' north. There's a lot I like about the South. The weather ain't too bad except in the middle of summer. Most people are really nice too, at least up on Monte Sano. And there's Jude and you, of course. But, in the end, once you come down off the mountain, it's all these damn separation rules that git to you after a while. One day a white person will be as sweet as honey to you and the next thing you know you gotta drink out of a certain water fountain, move over to the outside when they walk by you on the sidewalk, sit way up in the balcony with the whores at the Opera House, not speakin' till you been spoke to, and all this yassuhing and nosuhing all the time. It's just too degrading and complicated and wearing and even dangerous, if you make a misstep, trying to keep up with it all. I don't think I can do it much longer."

"I guess I can't blame you," she says. "You should hear Grandmama spout about how it was back in slavery days. She says the white man was and still is the ruler of everything, that the white man throws down a load and tells the colored man to pick it up, and he picks it up, but he don't tote it — instead he hands it to his womenfolks. Grandmama says the colored woman is the mule of the world. And then Daddy joins in and says it ain't nothing hardly changed since we been free. We's still poor and still beholden to white folks and still slavin' away like always. He says we'd be up north right now, if we had any family or knew anyone up there. But everybody and everything we know is right down here in this poor little racist backwater of a town."

"So what are you gonna do about it, when you git old enough?"

"I don't know. I'm hopin' we can scratch together enough money so's I can study botany at the State Normal and Industrial School and then see what happens. Maybe I'll come up north with you."

"I'd like that," I tell her. "I'd like that a lot."

Vanishing Falls

Periwinkle Spring

CHAPTER TWENTY FOUR

DEAR DIARY,

EVER SINCE INDEPENDENCE DAY, Mama has been quizzing me about Jude. Like I told Jude, she has a way of seeing right through me about most everything. So I've been telling her the truth, for the most part. I've told her I like him, which I guess was obvious to her anyway, but I haven't told her that we've been getting together most every day or that we've been kissing and cuddling and carrying on like that.

She would have us packing for home right away, if she knew that. As it is, she said that she and Papa are still concerned about our safety, especially since the murderer hasn't been found yet, even though the sheriff is still questioning a bunch of people.

I saw Clara at the baseball game on the Fourth of July. We talked while the boys played. She said that she can tell that Jude really likes me by the way he looks at me. She said that Jude tried to spike her cousin John because he was jealous of him, but Jude said it was just about baseball. I still don't understand the game, even though Clara tried to explain it to me. She's all excited about this big ball that General Moore is throwing on July 21 downtown, and she wants me to go to it with her and spend the night with her in town. I don't know if Mama will go for that, but I told Clara I would try to convince her.

I've managed to keep Jeremy quiet about going back home early. I've been buying him candy at the news stand in the lobby and playing croquet and lawn tennis with him whenever he wants. This gives Mama a break too, so she can sit out on the porch by herself and enjoy the view, the breeze, and a good book. And usually by the time Jeremy and I get back to the room after playing whatever games he wants to play, Mama is also enjoying a pre-dinner glass, or two, of sherry. So I figure if I can keep Mama happy and Jeremy quiet and Jude out of Mama's sight and we can find the murderer, my chances of staying until the end of summer are pretty good. But that's a lot of "ifs." So we shall see.

The first couple of weeks since we arrived here were cool and often rainy, but now it's turned hot and muggy. I've asked Jude to take me swimming, but he's been so busy in the stable now that Sherm's dead that he hasn't had time. Besides, the only two swimming holes nearby are at Fagan Spring, where they're usually a lot of people, and the more isolated Periwinkle Spring where Jude says some big boulders have dammed up the little creek that flows from the spring to make a pool where you can at least cool off. The only trouble is you have to scramble down a steep, rocky hill to get to the bottom of McKay Hollow where the spring is.

"By the time you get there, you're ready for a swim," Jude said, "and by the time you get back up the hill, you're ready for another one."

But today was so sweltering that I couldn't stand it any longer. Mama took Jeremy into Huntsville on the train because he has outgrown most of his light cotton summer clothes and she needed to buy him some new shirts and knee pants. I was thinking about going with them, so I could see Clara, but I decided that it was just too damn hot, as Papa would say. So I left a note for Jude with Jim Robinson at the news stand, letting him know that I was going to go swimming in Periwinkle Spring and that he and Smokey were welcome to join me, if on the off chance they were able to get off work. I really didn't expect them to, and Jude had already showed me what path to take. So I got a lunch basket from Cook Cazzy and put my bathing suit and Mark Twain's new book, *A Connecticut Yankee in King Arthur's Court*, in with the food and took off, expecting to spend the day by myself, reading and cooling off in Periwinkle Spring.

The trail ran flat across the plateau from the hotel until it reached Carter Spring and then it dropped precipitously. And, besides being steep, it was rough and rocky. Not too far down was a cascading waterfall that was about a hundred feet high, not nearly as impressive as Niagara Falls, but still very pretty. The sign next to it identified it as Vanishing Falls. Jude told me earlier that it was called that because when it was dry there was no water at all flowing from it. There were beautiful views across the hollow, but it took a long time, maybe a couple of hours, to get to the bottom of it. I thought my toes were going to push through the tips of my boots the trail was so steep. By the time I finally got there it was past noon, and I was soaked with sweat. But it was cool and shady down there in that narrow, forested glade, with wildflowers blooming everywhere and cute, little lizards scurrying about over the rocks. And, sure enough, the little stream flowing out of the rocks had been dammed up enough by these two huge rocks to form a shallow pool, just deep enough for me to bathe in and cool off. So after I ate the roast pork sandwich, cucumber salad, and an apple that Cook Cazzy had packed, I found a couple of high rocks on the southern bluff just above the pool to hide behind and changed into my bathing suit. It was last year's and a little snug around my chest and hips, but the long black stockings and bloomers were mostly covered anyway by the black, knee-length wool dress and the white sailor-style collar. I figured no one was going to see me anyway, so I let down my hair and left my bathing slippers and cap in the picnic basket. And then I eased myself all the way in and sat on the pool's rocky bottom with only my head emerged. It was cool and glorious, and I must have relaxed in there for more than an hour, leaning my head back and staring up through the green trees into the dark blue sky above, as an eagle floated by, listening to the birds singing, and wishing Jude were there to enjoy it with me.

Finally, when he didn't show up, I stepped out of the water and sat on a rock to dry off while I read my book. I wasn't sure how long it would take me to climb up the bluff and back to the hotel, but I wanted to get back before supper, so Mama wouldn't have a conniption fit and another reason to take us back home early. So once I was almost dry, I went back behind the two high rocks where I had left my clothes and took off my bathing suit. And just as I had gotten completely naked, I heard voices coming down the path. I hurried to dress, but they couldn't see me behind the rocks anyway. But before I could get my bloomers up my damp legs, I recognized the voices. They were Jude and Smokey's, and, by the sounds of their footsteps and laughter, they were running down the path to the spring.

"Where's Sophie?" Smokey hollered.

"Don't see her. I guess she decided not to come. Last one in is a skunk's rump."

So, standing there with nothing but my bloomers halfway up my legs, I looked out through a crack between the rocks and what to my astonishment did I see, but Jude and Smokey stripping off their clothes: suspenders first, then shirts, trousers, and, oh my, under drawers. I didn't know what to do. I was so surprised and shocked, not to mention half naked myself, that I couldn't utter a word. And I know I should have at least turned away, but once my eyes were locked on them, I couldn't stop staring. Now, Mama has talked to me about sex and I have a little brother, so I do know the body parts of a boy, but I still wasn't prepared for what I saw, and I just couldn't make myself look away.

They were about twenty yards away and moving so fast that it was hard to focus. So as soon as they had all their clothes off they were in the water and, after a brief splashing fight, were sitting at the bottom of the pool on the rocks like I had. And, even though the water from the spring was clear, their bodies were sort of bleary under the cool water.

At this point, I didn't dare move to finish dressing or to escape or anything, for fear of them hearing me. So I stood there stupidly behind the rocks in my bloomers, holding my breath the best I could and staring agog at their naked bodies. And they were not at all as cute and tiny as Jeremy's, but instead rather odd and unexplainably arousing.

But once the novelty of these new, strange sights had subsided a bit, I relaxed a little and listened to them talk. And, let me tell you, it didn't take me long to confirm, as I eavesdropped on their conversation, what I had suspected for some time: boys are as stupid as mud. Because they basically talked about nothing: stuff about the baseball game on Independence Day, none of which made a bit of sense to me, their jobs and bosses and how tiresome they were, and nonsense about how they were going to be rich and famous when they were older.

I was completely dry when they finally got around to something good, namely girls.

"So what's going on with you and Ella Kendricks?" Jude asked Smokey. "I thought you said she had a boyfriend in town."

"Well, she did."

"Yeah, so what's goin' on?"

"Nothin'. She's just a little lonely, that's all. What about you and Little Miss?"

"You mean Sophie?"

"Yeah, I see she's got you meetin' the family."

"So?"

"You know the rule and you know what you promised me."

"So?"

"So when I arranged it for you to take her riding, you promised me you wouldn't get involved with her."

"What makes you think I'm getting involved with her?"

"Jude, don't lie to me."

"Okay, so I like her, so what?"

"Well, if Rogers finds out, he'll fire you; and if her mama finds out how much you like her, she's gonna pack Little Miss back home faster than a New York minute."

"That's why neither one of 'em are gonna find out."

"If you say so," Smokey sighed.

I thought those boys were going to shrivel up into prunes as long as they stayed in there, but finally they got out, and I breathlessly watched them dress and head back up the trail. So I finished dressing myself, and, when I couldn't see or hear them anymore, I started back up the steep path by myself. And, of course, it was much harder going up than coming down. Every time I thought I was at the top of the mountain, there would be another switchback and more rocks and more bugs and, the worst, more invisible spider webs spun across the trail, like icky, sticky veils across my face and hair.

I was beginning to think I was lost, but I knew if I kept going up that I would reach the top at some point. So I just kept going, sweating and swatting flies.

Then when I thought I could go no farther, I saw a black mass off to the side of the trail in a huckleberry thicket. I stopped and watched. The bear was sitting on the ground, his back to me, about ten yards from me and the trail, casually munching away on the red berries. I didn't know what to do — scream, run, or cry. So I froze, just hoping the bear wouldn't notice me, as it pulled a branch of the berries to its mouth and gobbled them up. I finally figured that the bear would decide to get up and move on at some point, and maybe the direction it would decide to move on in would be mine, so I slowly, quietly continued up the trail, with one eye on the bear and the other on the rocks on the trail. This would not be a good time to stumble. Even after I had gotten well past the bear, I kept looking back to make sure it wasn't following me.

By the time I finally got back to the hotel, Mama and Jeremy were already at supper. So I took a quick bath, changed into clean clothes, and joined them. When Mama asked why I was late, I told her the truth. Except I left out the part about Jude and Smokey and the bear.

Sophie Franklin
July 13, 1892

On Monte Sano

Wisdom Falls

CHAPTER TWENTY FIVE

THERE WAS NO CHURCH ON MONTE SANO. On the east side of Le Conte Street, Lucy Beirne Matthews had started building an Episcopal church in memory of her daughter Eliza. Back in February an Episcopal Bishop named Jackson had laid a cornerstone for the new mission. One side had these words carved in it: MAY 30th A.D. 1892 "SUFFER THE LITTLE CHILDREN COME UNTO ME AND FORBID THEM NOT FOR SUCH IS THE KINGDOM OF GOD." Another side read: THE CHURCH OF THE HOLY INNOCENTS "OUT OF THE MOUTH OF BABES AND SUCKLINGS THOU HAST PERFECTED PRAISE." And the third gray granite side was decorated with two ornate flowers and a Celtic cross, with the words: JESUS CHRIST THE CHIEF CORNER STONE.

But only about six feet of the walls surrounding this elaborate stone had been completed so far. So on summer Sunday mornings, those who were so inclined met on the porch of the Hotel Monte Sano or at someone's house, like Uncle Matt's, who hosted the service this week. Occasionally a traveling clergyman of one denomination or another would show up and, in exchange for Sunday dinner and the proceeds from the morning's collection plate, preside over the services, but usually the participants conducted a rather free-form type of worship, with hymn-singing, prayers, bible reading, and testimonials at the whim of those present.

Jude and his daddy usually attended, as well as a few other hotel staff and a number of guests at the Hotel Monte Sano, including the

159

Franklin family. On the third Sunday in July, an itinerant Baptist preacher, named Reverend Floyd Boyd, with an unruly thatch of red hair and a large gold watch fob, showed up and took charge of the service. He turned out to be a stern and serious man, who prayed long and hard and then steadily gathered steam on a long and loquacious sermon about the sin of lust, which struck Jude a bit too close to home. He didn't know how Sophie was taking it, because all he could see was the neat bun on the back of her head, but he had a feeling she was wincing and feeling as guilty as he was.

When the service ended, Jude was relieved and regretful, but it didn't keep him from ditching his daddy and taking off to see Sophie at Wisdom Falls, the place where they had agreed to meet. He leaned against a large poplar and watched the water fall over the rocks, waiting for her, but not for long.

"That was brutal," Sophie gasped, as she ran to him.

"It was almost like he's been watching us," Jude said.

"Maybe he has."

"Geez, I hope not. We'll both go to hell for sure."

"Well, at least we'll be together," Sophie laughed.

"Yeah, burning together forever."

"Where's Smokey?"

"I don't know. I told him we'd meet him here after church, but maybe Mr. Denison sent him on a chore or something."

"Well, until he gets here …"

So, despite the preacher's recent admonitions, they proceeded to do precisely what he had warned them so fervently not to do. As the summer progressed, so did their spooning. And even though they knew that they should stop, before they went too far, they just couldn't seem to keep their hands off of each other.

But when they heard Smokey coming, they quickly separated. However, Smokey knew by their disheveled clothes, flushed faces, and embarrassed looks what had been going on. "Okay, break it up," he said. "You know, sooner or later the wrong person is gonna see y'all carryin' on."

"Like the Baptist preacher who condemned us to eternal damnation this morning?"

160

"What?"

"Never mind."

"Who wants a sandwich? Cook Cazzie made some for us."

Smokey passed out smoked ham sandwiches and they sat on the ground and ate them under the spreading poplar tree among the old, gray rocks, listening to the cool water rush over the limestone cliff like a soothing serenade. A whippoorwill trilled somewhere overhead and a light breeze blew through the leaves.

"So you really think we can do better than the sheriff in finding out who slit Sherm's throat?" Smokey asked, since Jude had told him all about Sophie's idea that they should try to find the murderer.

"Well, I don't know," Sophie said. "Probably not. All I know is that it's likely that I'm gonna have to go back to Schenectady sooner rather later unless someone finds him; and so far, the sheriff doesn't seem to be doing too good. I just don't feel like sitting around on my hands, when we could be doing something."

"Like what?" Jude asked.

"Well, among the three of us, we pretty much know everyone around here, don't we? Jude, you know everyone in the stable and all the folks who live in the cottages on the mountain. Smokey, you know everyone else who works in the hotel. And I know a lot of the guests. So we should have it covered. Who do you think killed him?"

"What if it was someone who doesn't work or live up here, like that poker-player guy, Comstock?" Smokey asked.

"Then we're out of luck," Sophie said.

"Well, anybody got any bright ideas?" Smokey asked.

"Well, I didn't tell the sheriff," Jude said, "but apparently someone else did, because the sheriff told Mr. Denison that he knew Rogers and Sherm didn't get along."

"So you think Rogers killed him?" Sophie asked.

"Nah, Rogers doesn't get along with anyone. There's no reason that I know of he would've killed Sherm, other than anyone else."

"Well, let's keep him on the list of possibilities anyway," Sophie said. "Who else?"

"I didn't tell the sheriff," Smokey said, "but I've been thinking about it. A few weeks ago I overheard an argument between Colonel O'Shaughnessy and some man he called Jay. This Jay guy was trying to git O'Shaughnessy to sell the hotel to some investors from South Dakota, and he mentioned how someone falling off the bluff could ruin business at the hotel. So maybe this Jay guy arranged for Sherm to git killed so that O'Shaughnessy would sell the hotel."

"Hmm … sounds like he goes on the list too," Sophie said. "Who else?"

"I was sort of wondering about that strange man you saw sharpening a knife down in McKay Hollow, the new man who works for Major Scrimshaw," Jude said to Smokey. "What's his name?"

"Will," Smokey answered. "He's a strange one alright. I had a run-in with him a while back that I didn't tell no one about. I was out looking for Scrimshaw so the sheriff could question him, and I run across him. He was hacking a rattler to death with a rake over by O'Shaughnessy's lily pond. He was real nasty with me and called me names. But I don't know if he's wacky enough to kill somebody."

"What about the knife?" Sophie asked.

"I saw him sharpening a big ol' knife in a little creek halfway down to McKay Hollow — I told Jude about it — and he cut himself with it and started laughing like crazy."

"On the list," Sophie said. "Who else?"

"I can't think of anyone else," Jude said. "How about any guests? Any of them suspicious?

"No," Sophie said, "not that I can think of, except for the Comstock man who grabbed Jeremy on the train, and he's gone. But I'll start being more on the lookout. Jude, why don't you keep an eye on Rogers and see if you can find out anything more about him and Sherm. And, Smokey, why don't you check up on this Jay fellow. See what more you can find out about him. How about Scrimshaw's man Will?"

"Don't look at me," Smokey said. "The man's got it in for me. He ain't gonna give me the time of day."

"Okay," Sophie said. "I'll see what I can find out. Those gardeners are always hanging around the hotel, weeding and pruning and stuff. I'll find out which one he is and try to talk to him."

"Oh," Jude remembered, "Sheriff Murphy told Mister Denison in the carriage on Independence Day that he was hoping to find out more about Sherm, who was from Moulton over in Lawrence County, from the sheriff over there. And he said he was going to check with the police in Louisville where Comstock said he was from. So, Smokey, see if you can hear anything more about that, willya?"

"Sure."

"And one more thing …" Sophie said.

"Yeah?"

"Everybody be careful."

Memphis Row

CHAPTER TWENTY SIX

DEAR DIARY,

SMOKEY FOUND OUT from Mr. Denison that the odd man Will's last name was Brock and pointed him out to me. He's a wiry little man with unruly black hair and a straw cowboy hat who looks sort of like an Indian to me — ruddy complexion, straight nose, and dark brown eyes. He was down on his knees, pulling weeds out of the garden next to Memphis Row, when I approached him.

"Excuse me, sir, are you Will Brock," I asked him.

"Huh?"

"Are you Mr. Brock?"

"Yes, ma'am," he answered with a wary look in his eyes. "What can I do fer ya?"

"Well, you look awful familiar to me," I lied, trying to figure out what to say next. "Could you tell me where you're from?"

"Uh …" he muttered and spit brown tobacco juice on the ground. "Not from around here."

"Where then?"

"Indian Territory, Oklahoma Territory, Texas, around there."

"What brought you here, if you don't mind me asking."

"Work. I heard there was work to be had here."

"You don't have family around here then?"

"No, why you askin'?"

"Just wondering. You look sorta like a man I met over in Moulton."

"In Moulton, huh? Don't know no one in Moulton."

"Oh, well. I'm sorry," I said, as the man stared at me with those narrow, dark eyes. So I turned to leave, but decided to try one more time. "Oh, one more thing," I said. "You don't by any chance know the man who was killed up here a couple weeks ago do you?"

Then this Will fellow really gave me a look, an angry look that shot through me like a lightning strike, and then he spit again. I was afraid for a minute that I was going to start crying, but I just lowered my eyes and started backing away.

Finally, he said, "No, I don't know the man. I have work to do. Leave me alone."

So I don't know where to go from here. Even if the man is telling the truth, he scares the hell out of me, as Papa would say. So I'm just going to stay away from him.

Mama has not mentioned going home for a while. It seems like as long as I keep Jeremy out of her hair and she has a few drinks each evening, she's okay with us staying. Of course, Jeremy continues to be a colossal pain. Yesterday, he chased a raccoon into the woods, and I had to go after him, so he wouldn't get lost. We both got tangled up in some kind of brier patch and came out with a bunch of nasty scratches all over us. But I guess I'll keep playing with him as much as I can stand, and, of course, seeing Jude a little while every day after supper.

Last night, I had another visit from Malinda Rowe. She was standing at the end of Jeremy's bed like the last time, and she seemed content to just stare at me there in the dark for the longest time. I didn't know what to say to her. I was too afraid to say anything. Finally, she smiled and whispered, "You are a very brave girl."

"I am?"

"Yes," she said. "You're trying to find a killer so you can stay here with your lover and … me."

"Well, I'm not doing very a very good job of it so far. I haven't found out anything yet. Do you know who murdered that man?"

"Yes," she answered.

"You do? Who?"

"I can't tell you," she answered with a faint grin. "You'll have to find out for yourself."

166

"Is he still around here, close by?"

"Yes," she said. "Very close by. But be careful. He's very dangerous. Maybe you should come with me." Then she held her hand out to me. I shook my head. And then she vanished as quickly and quietly as she had appeared.

Sophie Franklin
July 18, 1892

The Barn

CHAPTER TWENTY SEVEN

JUDE FOUND AN OLD ABANDONED BARN on what was once the Clay property, not too far from the hotel. Colonel O'Shaughnessy owned the property now, but the barn still stood, somewhat awkwardly due to its age, back in an untended apple orchard and overgrown garden. Even though it had some leaks, it was a fairly dry place for Jude and Sophie to meet on rainy afternoons, after supper, when their usual meeting places outside had turned too wet and muddy.

Jude arrived first and spread the saddle blanket he had brought over the straw in the corner. Besides the pile of straw the only thing left in the barn was an old, broken-down, wooden wheelbarrow half filled with red dirt. He peaked through the crack in the door that he had left partially open and soon saw her racing through the orchard toward him.

"Did you get wet?" he asked her, as she ran to him and hugged him.

"A little," she laughed.

"Where did you tell your mama you were going?"

"To the news stand to get a magazine, so we don't have much time. I'll have to stop by the news stand on my way back and find something."

Jude led her to the saddle blanket and pile of straw. They lay there together and snuggled as the rain beat gently on what was left of the barn's tin roof. Occasionally a drop would fall on one of them.

"Do you think we're going to hell for lying to our parents?" Sophie asked.

"Probably."

"Doesn't that bother you?"

"What, going to hell?"

"Yeah."

"Lying is probably the least of my sins," Jude whispered. "So I'm going to hell, if there is such a place, whether I keep on lying or not. But if you're asking me if I feel bad about lying, especially to my daddy, sure, I do, but sometimes you gotta do what you gotta do. Maybe, I figure, sometimes it's better to lie than to get your parents all worked up and worried about something they shouldn't be that concerned about."

"You don't think our parents should be concerned about what we're doing?"

"What are we doing?" Jude asked.

"Well, that's a good question. We're doing an awful lot of touching, don't you think?"

"So what's wrong with that?" Jude asked, as he pushed his hand up under her blouse.

"Well," she sighed, "If you put it that way. It does feel awfully good. So I'm not sure there's anything really wrong with it. Though our parents probably wouldn't see it that way, and ..."

"And what?"

"And ... I don't want to get pregnant."

"I know," he said and kissed her.

They continued to snuggle as the rain increased. Jude did feel bad that he had so little will-power when it came to loving her like this. So when she finally pushed him away, both of them gasping and flushed, he was both glad and sad.

"What do we do now?" he asked her.

"About what?"

"About us?"

"I don't know."

"Is your mama still talking about going back to Schenectady?"

"Sometimes ... but apparently Papa has been so wrapped up in this merger thing that he hasn't had time to pressure Mama much. To tell you the truth, as long as I keep Jeremy out of her hair and give her a few drinks every night, I think she's perfectly happy staying right where she is."

"That's good. What about her suspicions about you and me?"

"She knows," Sophie said. "I go off every night after supper by myself and come back all happy and glowing. She's gotta know."

"So what does that mean?"

"I'm not sure. On the one hand, I think she likes to see me happy, but on the other, I'm just waiting for her to call it all off and say that's enough and take us back home. Maybe I'm just feeling guilty, but every night when I come back to our room, I'm afraid she's gonna realize what we've been up to and tell me to start packing. That's why I think we should try to find Sherm's murderer. So she'll have one less reason to make us leave here early."

"Okay," Jude said, as he rolled over on top of her.

CHAPTER TWENTY EIGHT

JUNIOR HAD NO TROUBLE *getting a job at the Hotel Monte Sano. Dishwashers and gardeners came and went, and Major Scrimshaw hired him with little concern for his experience or past. After all, anybody could pull weeds and mow grass, which is what Junior did pretty much every day, except when it rained; then he cleaned, sharpened, or oiled tools, whatever Scrimshaw told him to do. He lived quietly in a corner of the toolshed under the hotel's first-floor porch and took his meals with the other hotel employees in the servants kitchen. He made enough to buy himself an occasional bottle of whiskey from the bartender at the hotel's saloon, and he sipped it after supper every night until he passed out and fell asleep.*

On Sundays, his day off, Junior monitored the movements of Sherm Williams who worked in the stable. Williams worked some Sundays, but had most of them off. Junior couldn't figure out the pattern, if there was one. He only knew that if Williams was not working, he would do about the same thing every Sunday. First, he would have breakfast with the other servants in the kitchen, then he would go to church, and afterward he would eat dinner. In the afternoon, he would do his laundry in the hotel laundry and hang his clothes out to dry. Then he would walk to Ella's Rock and stare out over the valley and watch the sun set over the Tennessee River. And then he would walk back to the kitchen for supper. And after supper, he would take his clothes off the line, put them in a basket, and return to the stable. It was the same routine every Sunday, unless it rained. Then he spent most of the day in the stable, playing cards or dominoes with the other men who worked there.

Since Williams spent the evening hours in the stable, Junior figured the best time was the twilight hour when he walked back to the hotel from Ella's Rock. Most people were finished with the day's activities by then and were heading to the dining room to eat supper.

So on the clear, steamy last Sunday in June, Junior again followed Sherm Williams on his day off — to the servants kitchen for breakfast, to church on the hotel's porch, back to the kitchen for dinner, then to the laundry, and finally to Ella's Rock. Junior found an isolated, wooded spot along the path between Ella's Rock and the hotel. He located a sharp drop off the bluff. He crouched behind a cross-vine thicket and waited. And, as the sun slowly sunk into the valley, he thought about his pa and his big brother and how they had been killed. He still remembered well the sight of his pa, swinging helplessly from the old hickory tree in their front yard. He was ready now for the final revenge.

So when Williams was returning from Ella's Rock and was two steps past him, Junior pounced. He wrapped his right arm across his chest and grabbed his shirt, and then, before Williams had a chance to react, with his left hand he swiped the razor-sharp blade across his neck. He heard the air rush from his severed windpipe and then the gurgle of blood as it filled his throat. His body soon went limp as the acrid blood drained from his brain, out the slit in his neck and over his chest and Junior's arm and onto the ground.

Junior dragged the body to the edge of the cliff and pushed it over the rim, but it did not fall as far as he had hoped. Williams' belt had somehow caught on a scrub cedar limb, holding his body in clear view of the trail. Junior momentarily thought of scrambling down the bluff and disengaging the body, so it could roll farther down and out of sight, but then he heard fast footsteps coming his way. So he ran along the bluff away from the hotel in the direction of Ella's Rock. Then he heard the scream and soon the commotion, so he stayed hidden in the woods until it was totally dark. He found the burlap bag of clean clothes that he had earlier stashed under Ella's Rock and he carried it to a nearby well, where he stripped and washed himself and his knife and put on the clean clothes from the bag. He folded the knife's blade into its bone handle and tucked it into the waist of his trousers, covered its top with his shirt, and cinched his belt tight. Then he stuffed the bloody clothes in the bag and dropped it down the well. He walked back to the toolshed and wrote a letter to his mother, telling her that she could now carve the eighth and final notch in the hickory stick that she had been saving lo these many years.

The sheriff came to the hotel to ask questions, but no one said a word to Junior about the murder. So he decided he would stay until the end of the summer so that he would not arouse any suspicion. He could save a little money and then in the fall, when the hotel closed, he could buy the makings of a whiskey still and go back to Whitman Creek and start another moonshine business.

But now this girl, a guest at the hotel, had come around, asking him questions, about where he was from, and who were his kin, and even if he knew the man who had been killed. He wasn't sure what she knew, but her sudden curiosity was making him nervous and afraid. So she left him no choice. He would have to do something about it.

A Trail on Monte Sano

The Stone Cuts

CHAPTER TWENTY NINE

DEAR DIARY,

JUDE KEPT TELLING ME about this amazing trail to something he called the Stone Cuts. He said Jeremy would love it, and, since I was running out of new things to do with the little monster, I decided to take him there. So, this morning, when Jude was working and Mama wasn't feeling well, I got directions from Jude's daddy at the front desk, and a basket lunch from Cook Cazzy in the kitchen, and Jeremy and I set out to follow the trail that Mr. Schrimsher had directed us to.

First we cut across the top of the mountain, due east of the hotel, following a path that at first paralleled the railroad tracks. But when the tracks curved sharply north along the top of the ridge, we followed a steep trail down into what a sign at the top said was Mills Hollow. There were a lot of switchbacks and Jeremy was having great fun running back and forth ahead of me down into the bottom of the hollow. I was just hoping he wouldn't trip on a rock and fall down and break his leg or something, because it was going to be hard enough as it was going back up.

At the bottom of the hollow were a series of sinkholes, apparently caused by the rainwater rushing down the now dry streambeds from the top of the mountain and into this beautiful valley with a dense forest of trees that Jude had taught me the names of: pin and live oak, silver and red maple, sassafras, hickory, basswood, locust, and tulip trees draped in flowing veils of green muscadine vines.

Then the trail looped up and up, like a long, wriggling, craggy snake. Both Jeremy and I were panting by the time we arrived at the stone cuts at the top of the ridge. We had a beautiful view of the valley on the other side of the ridge and of the hollow we had just emerged from. Then we entered a stone wonderland where it looked like a series of huge, high rocks had been slivered into a long labyrinth of tight limestone lanes. These rock walls towered about a hundred feet above us on both sides of the narrow trail that wove through them. Then we entered a short tunnel formed by the rock walls on either side of us and huge boulders across the top. After that, we entered another slender chamber, dripping with water from somewhere above. Jeremy couldn't get enough of it, squeezing through the slim passageway before me, and then popping out to scare me, as we found our way through.

When I was finally able to get Jeremy out of there, we climbed even higher along the ridgeline and up through a jumble of giant boulders to the top of what the sign identified as Panther's Knob. At the summit, called Logan Point, was another spectacular view of the valley below and the surrounding mountains. A huge rock balanced on another rock, like a giant shoe. Jeremy and I sat on the rock outcropping and enjoyed the view and Cook Cazzy's lunch: cheese sandwiches, cold slaw, sliced carrots, and apples, as well as Cook Cazzy's sweet and tangy lemonade that tasted marvelous.

Then it was down again, back into Mills Hollow. Jude told me there was a cave called Teakettle Cavern somewhere around there, but I couldn't find it. We followed a dry streambed that led to another big sinkhole, and then it was climbing time again to get back to the top of Monte Sano and the hotel. By this time, Jeremy had had enough. He moaned and groaned as we ascended the steep trail, constantly asking me how much farther it was to the top.

As we huffed and puffed our way up, Jeremy stumbling in front of me, I got the distinct sense that we were being followed, but every time I turned around to check, I couldn't see anything. Then when the sun started to drift below the treetops on the cliff above, I heard a limb snap above us.

"What was that?" Jeremy asked.

I jerked around, but I still couldn't see anything out of the ordinary. But I knew something was there. "Who's there?" I called.

There was no answer, so I told Jeremy to hurry up. We continued as fast as I could push Jeremy up the steep trail, looking desperately for the summit. By now we were both drenched in sweat, and I was near tears in fright. I was sure something was stalking us and I feared it was getting closer by the minute. And, if I had had any more strength, I would have tried to get Jeremy to run with me away from there, but I was just too exhausted. Finally, Jeremy stopped, plopped himself down on a rock, dropped his head between his legs, and announced that he could go no farther.

I pleaded with him, telling him that we had no choice. We had to continue to the top or spend the night here. I didn't tell him that I was sure we were being followed, but I warned him that there were wild animals out here. He just sat there and whimpered. I didn't know what to do, so I just stood there, helplessly, shamed by my fleeting thought of just leaving him there in the woods by himself and running away from whatever or whoever was coming after us.

After a while, I turned to look up into the rocks to see if I could see the top, and then I saw our pursuer, crouched on a flat overhang, about thirty feet away, its two round, dark eyes silently watching us. I turned away and began to shake.

Jude had told me that some men had followed a panther that had carried off a young pig near the burnt-out Fearn/O'Shaughnessy house, but I thought it was just another one of Jude's stories. But now I was face to face with one of them, and I had no idea what to do. At first glance, it looked like nothing more than an overgrown house cat, but then I saw its paws, wide and brown with long, sharp claws, its spooky, glaring eyes, and the smooth, poised muscles of its shoulders and front legs.

I looked at Jeremy who sat motionless, his head still down between his legs, a few feet closer than I was to the panther. And I was too scared to warn him. I was too tired to run, too intrigued to cry, and too afraid to scream. So I bowed my head to pray and tried to think of pure, clean last thoughts. But my thoughts were mostly of Jeremy and me being torn to shreds by the panther's teeth and claws. When, after a while, we weren't, I peeked up to where the cat had sat and found that it had vanished, silently into the gathering darkness.

I gave Jeremy what little was left of Cook Cazzy's lemonade and that seemed to revive him. Two more switchbacks and we were on the summit, with a short walk back across the railroad tracks and the Monte Sano Pike and the flat, matte plateau, and finally to the hotel.

Mama was sitting on the porch in front of our room with a glass of sherry in her hand when we returned, and Jeremy began to tell her about our hike. And, since I didn't think our encounter with the panther would help my argument to stay longer at the hotel, I somehow forgot to mention that to her.

Sophie Franklin
July 19, 1892

Cold Spring Cave

Cold Spring

CHAPTER THIRTY

JUDE WAS CLEANING OUT Shadow's stall, while Shadow munched on his breakfast of hay and oats. Usually Jude cleaned the stall while the horses were out being ridden or in the pasture. But this morning, Mr. Rogers had ordered him to clean Shadow's stall while Shadow was still in it, because the vet was coming any minute to examine a sore on Shadow's fet lock. Jude had shoveled all the manure out and was splashing down the concrete floor with a bucket of water when a rat ran through the stall, right over Shadow's front hooves. Shadow jumped and kicked, hitting Jude on the bone just below his right knee. Jude cursed and went down hard on the concrete floor, wincing in pain. He wasn't sure if anything was broken or not, so he just lay there in Shadow's shadow, hoping that the ache would soon subside.

Apparently, Mr. Rogers had heard the commotion in the stall. He walked in and saw Jude lying on the floor. "Layin' down on the job again, I see. What happened?"

Jude explained.

"Well, git yo' sad ass up and git over to Doc Duffield, if you can," Rogers told him and walked away. Jude didn't know if he could stand up or not. Finally, Waya came in and helped him up, and he limped over to Doc Duffield's office in the hotel. The doctor examined his shin and declared it badly bruised, but not broken. So Jude limped back to work.

A few days later, Jude, Sophie, and Smokey met again, just before sunset, at Cold Spring. Jude and Sophie snuggled together on a bench in the gazebo, as Smokey paced restlessly back and forth in front of them. Sophie told them about her brief meeting with Will Brock and her two nocturnal encounters with Malinda Rowe's ghost.

"I ain't never seen a ghost," Smokey said. "Sure it wasn't just a dream?"

"Might have been," Sophie said. "It seemed real enough at the time, but I don't know for sure."

"See, I told you there was a ghost," Jude said. "So do you think this ghost or the man you talked to, who scared you, this Will Brock, may have had something to do with Sherm's murder?"

"I'm not sure," Sophie answered. "I think the ghost is probably harmless, even though she wants me to come with her to wherever she is. Will Brock said he was from out west somewhere — Oklahoma or Texas, I think he said. He said he didn't know anyone in Moulton or the dead man. But who knows if he was telling the truth or not. At any rate, there's something really weird about him. I don't know if he's a killer, but he sure is scary. What about you guys? Find out anything?"

"I got up enough courage to talk to Mr. Rogers about it, when I got back from the doctor," Jude said. "He told me that Sherm was a good horseman, despite their differences. That he was originally from over around Moulton, like we already knew, and that he apparently travelled around a lot and didn't ever stay too long in one place. Rogers said he got the impression that the man was running away from something, but he didn't know what."

"So do you think Rogers had anything to do with it?"

"Nah, I don't think so, but, if we could find out what Sherm was running away from, then maybe we'd know where to look next."

"I think I can tell you that," Smokey said.

"What?"

"First, let me tell you about this Jay guy. I talked to the colored butler at the O'Shaughnessy Place, Marcus Wilkens, and he told me the man was named Jay Gould and that he and the Colonel are old business buddies from way back. Gould owns a bunch of railroads and other stuff. Anyway, Marcus says Gould is dying of tuberculosis and has been comin' up to see the Colonel every summer since the hotel opened to see if the fresh air and water would help cure his TB. This Gould guy and the Colonel argue and fight like dogs, according to Marcus, but they're still big buddies."

"So could Gould have murdered Sherm?" Jude asked.

"Nah, I don't think so. Marcus said he thought Gould would gladly stab a man in the back to make a buck, but he doubted that he'd go as far as slitting a man's throat to best a buddy like the Colonel in business. Anyway, he had already gone back to New York, Marcus said, when Sherm was murdered."

"So … what else?" Sophie wanted to know.

"Well," Smokey said, "I've been listening every chance I get to Sheriff Murphy and Mr. Denison. The sheriff said that the Lawrence County sheriff had asked around over there and found out what Sherm was running away from was a family named Brooks. He said that in Moulton everyone is afraid of this family whose mother everybody calls Aunt Jennie. Seems that anyone who crosses her or her family is in for big trouble. But those in the biggest trouble of all are members of a bunch called the Lawrence County Home Guard."

"What's that?"

"Well," Smokey answered, "I ain't exactly sure, but, from what the sheriff said, I figure it was these men who helped the Confederate army find soldiers back during the War Between the States. They was sort of like this ragtag police force that went around recruiting soldiers, finding deserters, and killing anyone who helped the enemy. Anyway, near the end of the War, this bunch tried to get Aunt Jennie's husband and her oldest son to join the Confederate army. And when they refused, this so-called home guard killed both the Brooks father and his son. Aunt Jennie found out who was in this home guard, and she and her other sons set out to get revenge. And, according to the sheriff, she and the boys have done a pretty good job of it, cause every one of the eight men that killed her husband and son have been killed, except for one that went missing ever since the others started being killed. And I'll give you one guess who the one was that went missing."

"Sherm Williams," Sophie said.

"Bingo!" Smokey said.

"So this Aunt Jenny killed Sherm?" Jude asked.

"Well, not likely," Smokey said, "since she's an old woman by now and, according to Sheriff Murphy, doesn't get around too good anymore."

"So one of her sons?" Sophie asked.

"That's what the sheriff figures, but the trouble is he don't know how many's left or where they're at. No one does, except maybe Aunt Jennie, and she ain't tellin'."

"So where does that leave us?" Jude asked.

"I'm not sure," Sophie said. "What's the sheriff intend to do now, Smokey?"

"He told Mr. Denison that if the man just came up here and slit Sherm's throat and then took off, like this Comstock fellow, we may never find him. But, if the man was still around, as a guest or employee, then maybe we could catch him."

"How?"

"I don't know," Smokey said. "That's when Mr. Denison told me to get fresh cups of coffee for him and the sheriff."

"What about Comstock?"

"The sheriff said that the police in Louisville didn't have a record of anybody by that name."

"So he's just disappeared?"

"I guess so," Smokey said. "The sheriff said he was gonna telegraph the authorities in Birmingham, Memphis, Nashville, Chattanooga, and Atlanta to see if they knew anything about the man, but the sheriff said that was gonna take some time."

"Do you think we should tell the sheriff about this Will Brock character?" Sophie asked.

"I don't know," Jude said. "The fact that he's a little weird and scares you probably won't be enough to make the sheriff do anything."

"I don't know what to do," Sophie said.

"Let's me and you, Jude, keep an eye on this Will fellow," Smokey suggested. "I'll ask around, see if Scrimshaw or someone knows anything more about him. Meanwhile, you stay away from him, Sophie."

So they left it at that, but the three of them looked at each other with an uneasy sense of dissatisfaction. They didn't know where or who, but there was a murderer out there somewhere — nearby if the ghost of Malinda Rowe was right — and that left them troubled, shaken, and more than a little afraid of what they might discover next.

Court House Square

CHAPTER THIRTY ONE

DEAR DIARY,

WHEN I RECEIVED the engraved invitation to attend the big Lily Flagg ball in Huntsville, it read:

IGNAL'S

Mr. Samuel H. Moore
requests the pleasure of your company,
Thursday evening, July the twenty first,
eighteen hundred and ninety two,
from nine to three o'clock.
Huntsville, Alabama.

Complimentary
to
Signal's Lily Flag, the Jersey cow of the world
One year's record,
Butter 1047 pounds. ¾ ounces.
Milk 11339 pounds.
Winner of the Derby of the Jerseys against
the great Bisson's Belle.
Record,
Butter, 1028 pounds, 15 ⅝ ounces.
Milk, 8412 pounds, 7 ounces.

R.S.V.P.

Enclosed in the envelope was a note from Clara Matthews asking if I could go to the party with her and also stay the night at her house only a few blocks away, owing to the late hour of the party. I showed the invitation and Clara's note to Mama. She read them over a couple of times and said, "I've only met Clara once, at the dance here last month, and, while she seems nice enough, I'm not sure I know her well enough for you to go to this party and then spend the night with her. And it seems like maybe this is a grown-up affair, it being so late and all, maybe a bit too adult for you."

"Oh, please, Mama," I begged. "Clara said it will be the biggest bash Huntsville has ever seen, and it's going to be so much fun. How can I miss it? And I'm almost sixteen."

"Well, let me talk to Mr. Denison," Mama said, "to see what he knows about this party and Clara's family."

So at dinner that night, Mama asked Mr. Denison to dine with us at our usual table near the wide window overlooking the bluff. After Mama had explained the situation to him, he smiled, straightened his regimental stripe tie, and said, "I completely understand your concern. These young people sometimes get a bit carried away in their eagerness to become adults, sometimes well before we wish they would. But, I can assure you, in this case, your concerns are unfounded. The Matthews are an old and well-respected family in Huntsville, and, as far as I know, Clara is a fine young lady. And, as far as the party goes, General Moore is a rich, young bachelor who likes to entertain, so I'm sure the party will be lavish and great fun. There will however be plenty of adult supervision, the Matthews and myself included. I'm going not only to enjoy myself, but also to see that the hotel guests who are attending enjoy themselves too, but not too much, if you know what I mean. So I'll be keeping an eye on Miss Sophie, if you should allow her to attend. Or, if you prefer, I'm sure I could procure an invitation for you, Mrs. Franklin."

"No, that won't be necessary," Mama said. "One — what should I call it? — cowlebration is good enough for me, but I'll keep thinking about whether Sophie can go."

"Oh, please, Mama!"

Two days later, we received a message in our mailbox in the lobby. It was from Clara's mother inviting Mama and me for tea on the afternoon of the party. Mrs. Matthews suggested that we ride down on the two-forty-five train and join her and Clara at their house, then Mama could take the six o'clock train back up the mountain, if she didn't want to attend the party, and Mrs. Matthews would chaperone Clara and me and see that I got on the one-thirty train back the day after the party. So after I begged some more, Mama finally wrote a note back, saying that would be fine.

Meanwhile, Jude and the rest of the men who work in the stable are completely booked with taking hotel guests into Huntsville for the party. So I don't know when or if I'll see him tonight. Jude said that he had to stay with the horses and carriages at General Moore's stable during the party until Mr. Rogers ordered him to take someone back up to the hotel.

Just a few hours ago, Mama left Jeremy with one of the hotel's baby sitters, and she and I rode the train into Huntsville to have tea with Clara and Mrs. Matthews. As it had on Independence Day, the train backed down the mountain, since there was nowhere for it to turn around on Monte Sano. And what to our surprise, there was Clara and her mother and a Negro man waiting for us in the depot's waiting room in downtown Huntsville. Clara ran up to me, and everyone introduced themselves. Mrs. Matthews, who is beautiful, was dressed like Clara, in a long, white cotton dress with a blue satin sash around her waist.

"Even though it's hotter than Hades," Mrs. Matthews said, "we thought we would give you a quick tour of downtown Huntsville, if you don't mind. It's only a few blocks to our house on Eustis, but, if we walk down Jefferson Street, you can see most of the town. James here can take Sophie's valise straight to our house, so she doesn't have to lug it."

So we walked down Church Street and took a left on Arms to Jefferson Street, where a sign identified the big building on the northeast corner as the Huntsville Cotton Mill. Not more than a block farther on Jefferson was a handsome, two-story, red brick building, with three wide arched doors on the first floor. "That's the City Scales and Engine House Number One," Mrs. Matthews informed them. "There is no Engine House Number Two, yet, so it's someone in City Hall's wishful thinking, I assume."

We continued on the narrow sidewalk, shaded by live oaks and Spanish moss, past the Colored Methodist Episcopal Church and School, and, over on Washington, we saw the Penson and Pierce Livery Stable, where Jude and I had gone to get the carriage after the baseball game on the Fourth of July.

"There's St. Mary's across the street," Mrs. Matthews pointed out, "a beautiful little Catholic church built in what I believe they call the Romanesque Revival style. It's made of native limestone, all cut and hauled by mule carts from Monte Sano. It was completed back in 1872. Oh, look! There's Father Tracy coming down the steps now. Hi, Father."

Mrs. Matthews smiled and waved at the short, beaming man bouncing down the church's steps in long, black clerical robes. "Good afternoon to you," he yelled, with a slight Irish lilt, and waved. "Praise be to God for this beautiful day. May He bless you and keep you."

"And there's the Temple Emmanuel down the street," Mrs. Matthews pointed out. "We now have several fine Jewish families in town who are especially active in Huntsville's charitable activities."

A block and a half farther on, we came to a busy street corner with three large buildings looming above. "This, along with the Courthouse Square, is pretty much the center of Huntsville," Mrs. Matthews said. "On this corner here at Clinton Street, you have the McGee Hotel, City Hall, and the Opera House. The hotel was owned by Henry McGee up until his untimely death last month. Guess what his last words were?"

"I don't know," Mama said.

"Well, according to his widow, they were 'give me a drink of water,'" Mrs. Matthews laughed. "I hope I come up with something better than that when my time comes.

"The City Hall was completed in 1872 and was built out of this beautiful beige Monte Sano sandstone that was also used to build the new jail and many of the sidewalks around town. I believe it comes from a quarry on Round Top at the southern end of Monte Sano.

"We love the Opera House, don't we, Clara? I'm sure it's locked right now, but it's a big auditorium with hundreds of seats on the ground level and a balcony, supported by wooden piers, where they have three sections: one for poor white folks, one for Negroes, and another for harlots, who apparently enjoy the shows as much as the next person. I'm not sure how they know they're harlots, but that's what the sign in the ticket booth says. We've seen *The Gondolier's Opera* by Gilbert and Sullivan, and, let me see, what else? Oh yes, *The Streets of New York*, just a few months ago, and we always enjoy the Minstrel shows; Gorman's played here not too long ago."

Then we passed the Dewdrop Saloon, the W. R. Rison Bank, and some other stores, and then we were at the Courthouse Square. But it didn't look the same as it did on Independence Day, when it was crowded with people watching the parade. Now it was a normal business day. In the center, of course, was the imposing limestone courthouse, with its high dome and clock tower and solid white columns. Its shaded yard was encircled by a black, wrought-iron picket fence about five feet tall, and tied to the fence were horses and mules, either with saddles or harnessed to buggies, surreys, sulkies, wagons, and runabouts, many loaded with big bales of white cotton. Men hurried up the building's wide steps, others stood talking and smoking on the street corners, while more came and went through the swinging doors of the Huntsville Hotel Bar. Across the street were the Halsey Building and the new Farmers and Merchants National Bank. On the streets surrounding the square was a variety of stores and saloons: the A. F. Murray Books and Stationery Shop, Spotswood House, Campbell and Teetzel, and the Harrison Brothers Tobacco Store. Just a block off the square, on Eustis Avenue, we walked past the *Evening Tribune* office, a little grocery store, a combination sewing machine, piano and organ shop, and then the Church of the Nativity, its high copper steeple glistening in the afternoon sun. "Union soldiers were ordered to stable their horses in there," Mrs. Matthews said, "but when they read the inscription above the door, they refused the order."

"What does it say?" I asked.

"Follow me," Mrs. Matthews said, "and I'll show you."

So we followed her down the stone walkway to the church's entrance. And there carved into the stone above the church's double doors were the words: "Reverence My Sanctuary."

"And so they did," Mrs. Matthews said. "Of course, the prayers of the church's rector, dear Doctor Banister, probably didn't hurt matters either."

Then we passed the new red-brick Federal Building that was on the corner of Greene, Randolph, and Eustis Streets. "The Post Office is on the first floor," Mrs. Matthews told us, "and I'm proud to say that we now have free mail delivery all over town. Why, some of us — about thirty or so now — even have telephone service, if you can believe that. On the second floor is the federal court, and on the third there are jury rooms."

At the corner, Mrs. Matthews pointed down Greene Street. "On the next street over," she said, "at the corner of Gates and Greene is the old Weeden home. Miss Kate and her sister Miss Howard Weeden, two old maids, live there now. Miss Howard is a wonderful artist and poet who paints and writes about the darkies here in town. On any given Saturday you'll find her over on the square for Negro Day, the only white face in sight, gathering stories or painting portraits. Her parlor and dining room walls are covered with her work. Miss Kate loves to show the two-hundred and eight species of flowers from Monte Sano that Miss Howard painted last spring."

The Matthews' house was another block down on Eustis Avenue, just past the Y.M.C.A. building. "Our circulating library is in there," Mrs. Matthews said. "Our librarian Mrs. Betts does a fine job in keeping up with the latest literature."

Their house was a large two-story affair with white shutters and a tall, sprawling magnolia tree in the front yard which was surrounded by a white picket fence. Mrs. Matthews led us to the parlor where a colored maid served us tea and sponge cake. "Thank you so much for our tour of Huntsville," Mama said to Mrs. Matthews. "Now, tell me about yourself."

"Oh my, I don't know if there's that much to tell. I was born, just a few years before the War Between the States, and raised here in Huntsville. I married John when I was twenty and we have two children, Clara, who you know. She's sixteen now. And then we had Henry, who is three years younger than Clara. John, my husband, works downtown for the Thompson Land and Investment Company that buys and sells farm land in and around Huntsville. His brother William manages the Monte Sano Dairy. That's why we were invited to this party that Sam insisted on throwing. He says it's to publicize the dairy, but, truth be told, there is nothing Sam likes better than a good party, unless it's a good bottle of wine or a pretty girl. But don't worry; we won't let Sam near Sophie."

"Good," Mama said, while I just blushed and kept my mouth shut for once.

"So tell me more about this party tonight?"

"Well, it should be quite a shindig," Mrs. Matthews laughed. "Sam bought the house a few years ago, and it's a real showplace. It's a couple of blocks over on Adams. It was built by a man named Robert Watkins before the War. It has sixteen rooms, each with sixteen-feet high ceilings. And it has this beautiful black walnut woodwork throughout. There are three spiral staircases, one of which leads to a fancy cupola. According to people who were around when it was built, it took a Negro man named Charles Bell three years to construct them. One time Clara counted the windows in the house, and how many did you come up with, dear?"

"Fifty-eight all told," Clara answered. "Not to mention the nine doors it has that go to the outside."

"Sam's brought in porcelain bathtubs from New York," Mrs. Matthews continued, "marble mantels from Italy, and even converted the chandeliers to electricity, the first house to have it anywhere around here. So it takes quite a staff to keep the place up. But Sam has hired some of the best folks in town to do it. And just you wait, Sophie, to taste some of the pastries that Sam's colored cook, Zenie Pruitt, will be setting out tonight. She and her daughter and her two assistants, Tom Doregass and Charley Weeden, have been baking up a storm over there. Y'all be bustin' out of your gowns, for sure, before the night's over."

"My, my," Mama exclaimed. "But tell me more about Huntsville. We've been having a very relaxing time on Monte Sano, but I'm afraid we've not taken the time to get to know your town yet."

"Well, where to begin, before the War, and even after, it was not much," Mrs. Matthews said, "just a rural southern backwater. It was, and still is, mostly a farming and lumber community. We have about eight thousand people living here now. Cotton has always been king in these parts, but after the War Between the States, everything was a mess. We were relatively lucky here in Huntsville. The Union army didn't destroy everything, like they did in a lot of towns. So we survived, but it's never been the same. A lot of farms, plantations, and businesses went under. It hasn't been until recent years, with northern investment, that we've been able to grow much. Now, we have your Colonel O'Shaughnessy, Milton Humes, Oscar Goldsmith, W. W. Newman, the Chase Brothers, Jessie Moss, and a bunch of others who've come from up north to capitalize on all this cotton and to put Huntsville on the map. So there's the West Huntsville Cotton Mill, the Huntsville Cotton Mill Company, which we passed near the depot, one of the oldest cotton mills in the South, not to mention this huge new Dallas Mill that they're building in East Huntsville. And they say there're more to come."

"Sounds like quite a boom town," Mama said.

"Yes, well, I guess it is, for now, at least," Mrs. Matthews said. "Now tell me about yourself and Schenectady."

Then Mama went on and on about our family and Schenectady — about how Papa was an engineer who worked with Thomas Edison at the Edison General Electric Company that was merging with the Thomson-Houston Electric Company, about the Schenectady Locomotive Works, about the Erie Canal, and on and on — all pretty boring stuff, if you ask me. Frankly, I was glad when Mama finally stopped talking and left to catch the train back to Monte Sano, so Clara and I could start getting ready for the party.

First, Clara took me to the kitchen, where I was surprised to see Eliza, the colored woman who Jude had pointed out on Independence Day as his wet nurse, making supper for the family. Clara explained that, since the party didn't start until nine o'clock, we would have a light meal now to keep us all from starving. Eliza would serve Clara, her brother Henry, and me in the kitchen, and then serve Mr. and Mrs. Matthews in the dining room.

"Where's Henry?" Clara asked Miss Eliza.

"He's out back gittin' me more wood for the stove. Have you gals washed up yet?"

"Yes, ma'am," Clara lied.

"Then go wash up agin," Eliza instructed. "And y'all don't come back till you'se not got a speck of dirt under yo' fingernails."

Then Henry burst in with an armload of wood that he dropped in a tin tub next to the stove. He's a cute kid, about my size, with a ready smile and an easy laugh, so relaxed and free and not at all as annoying and aggravating as my brother Jeremy. Clara introduced him and Eliza to me.

"Sophie?" Eliza asked. "Are you the Sophie that's staying at the Monte Sano Hotel?"

"Yes, ma'am, I am. How'd you know?"

"Why, Jude told me all about you at the Fourth of July picnic," Eliza said with a grin. "That boy sure is stuck on you."

"He is?"

"Oh, I should say so. He jist went on and on about you, like you's as sweet as a slice of fresh apple pie. But you better be good to him, now, cause Jude ain't never had a galfriend before. So you treat him right, okay?"

"Yes, ma'am," I promised, as Eliza placed a platter of sliced, cured ham, a bowl of boiled potatoes, a plate of sliced tomatoes, and a loaf of light bread on the table. Everything was so good that I ate too much and was afraid I wouldn't be able to fit into my gown.

After we cleared the table, Clara and I went to her room to begin getting ready. First, I took a bath in their large porcelain bathtub. Clara said that less than a hundred families in Huntsville had indoor bathrooms, but they were running more pipes every day from the new reservoir on Echols Hill, just a few blocks over. Then Clara took a bath. Still in our heavy cotton robes, we went to Clara's room and laid out our clothes for the evening on her wide canopy bed.

The Hotel Monte Sano

Our combination chemise and drawers came first. Mama had bought me a white linen one with pretty blue satin ribbons. Clara put on a beige silk one with tons of lace. Then came our corsets. Clara had one with a bust bodice and bust improver, which I should have had, since I'm a lot flatter than she is, but Mama says I look fine just the way God made me. I'm not so sure about that. Next came the silky petticoats adorned with all kinds of frills and lace. I didn't count how many Clara put on, but I could only fit three into my valise, so that's what I wore. Finally, we squeezed into our floor-length gowns. Mine was made of fine white cotton, with a V-neck, short, puffy, leg-o-mutton sleeves, and a simple lace bodice. Clara's was beautiful, gold with blue trim, and a fancy embroidered bodice.   Our silk stockings and buttoned shoes completed our preparations, except for the hair. For that we went back downstairs to the kitchen, where Eliza was already warming the curling irons on the top of the stove. She worked expertly to form masses of ringlets on top of both of our heads. Then she went through a sewing basket full of ribbons and selected just the right one for each of us. "There," she said, tying the ribbons in place, "y'all will be the belles of the ball. Ain't no men gonna take their eyes offa y'all all night long. Too bad Jude won't be there to see y'all."

"Don't you think we should be wearing hats?" Clara asked her.

"Oh, no," Eliza answered. "Hats are fer ol' womens, like me, that's got somethin' to hide, like thin, stringy hair or a too-high hairline. Y'all ain't got nothin' to hide. Y'all's perfect jist the way you is."

Sophie Franklin
July 21, 1892

The Weeden House

General Moore's Mansion

CHAPTER THIRTY TWO

MANY OF THE HOTEL MONTE SANO'S GUESTS who were going to General Moore's big party for the jersey cow Lily Flagg were taking the train into town. Mr. Denison and Colonial O'Shaughnessy offered them the opportunity to stay in the Huntsville Hotel after the party for no additional charge. Some guests, however, preferred to go down the mountain via carriage or Tally Ho, either because they didn't trust the train or they found the horse-drawn means more picturesque. But Denison and O'Shaughnessy had apparently decided on a carriage because they wanted to talk in private, and, for some unknown reason, Mr. Rogers had assigned Jude to drive them to the party.

Riding down the turnpike at night could be a bit tricky, so Jude needed to be especially careful on the twisting road. Fortunately, there was a full moon and a cloudless sky, which made it so much easier. At first, the two talked about the hotel's finances. Jude couldn't follow it very well. They talked about a lot of numbers that didn't make much sense to him. But it was clear that the Hotel Monte Sano was not making as much money as it had before Sherm's death. Then, about half way down the mountain, Jude heard Colonial O'Shaughnessy ask Mr. Denison, "Anything new with the sheriff's investigation of the murder?"

"Not too much. Sheriff Murphy finally heard back from the police in Memphis, and they did have a record of this Bradley Comstock character who pulled a gun on Williams. He goes by a bunch of other names too, one of the more colorful being Magic Slim, if I remember correctly, but they said his real name was Morris Holt, I think. They said Bradley Comstock, Magic Slim, Cyrus Blackwell were a few of several aliases that this card shark used on the riverboats and casinos up and down the Mississippi River and now apparently here in Alabama. They said he had been accused of cheating more than once, but so far no one had ever proved it to be true. So he's either a really good card player or a really clever cheater. At any rate, they haven't seen hide nor hair of him in Memphis for several months now, but they doubt he's the one who killed Williams. He's never been arrested for anything so far, so they don't think he'd do anything as violent as slashing an innocent man's throat."

"What about Moulton?

"Well," Mr. Denison said, "Sheriff Murphy went over there, and he and the Lawrence County sheriff went out to this Aunt Jennie's place to ask her if she knew anything about the murder. And, as you would guess, she denied everything. She said she was glad he was dead, but she was busy delivering a baby the night Sherm Williams was killed. Apparently, she's a midwife over there."

"What about her sons?"

"The Lawrence County sheriff says they're mostly dead. One boy named Gainam killed a deputy a couple of years back and then was shot to death by a colored neighbor named Hubbard. One boy named Henry is in prison at Fort Leavenworth for stealing a horse. Another boy, Willis Junior, they think went out to Texas, Oklahoma, Indian Territory. Nobody's seen him for years."

For some reason, that sounded familiar to Jude, but he couldn't think of why. And the next thing that Colonel O'Shaughnessy said made him forget all about it. "Well, regardless of who murdered the man, I don't have to tell you how much the hotel's revenue has declined since he was murdered. As we just discussed, business at the hotel has fallen off badly during the past few weeks," he said. "And Jay Gould and others have convinced me that there is another financial panic coming, maybe as early as next year, so I've decided, along with the other stockholders, to go ahead and sell all the assets of the North Alabama Improvement Company, including the Hotel Monte Sano and the Huntsville Hotel, to a group of developers from Pierre, South Dakota, who are calling themselves the Northwest Land Association. I wanted you to be the first to know. I have no reason to believe that these new owners will not retain you and your staff, but, still, you should be aware."

"When?" Mr. Denison asked.

"Within the next few weeks. Certainly before the end of the season."

"Well … alright then, I guess there's nothing I can do about it. It's your property."

"I think, Harvey," Colonel O'Shaughnessy said, "that the only thing to do right now is to enjoy the evening."

And the rest of the ride to town was very quiet, as Mr. Denison — and Jude — contemplated their future.

Soon after passing the Cumberland Presbyterian Church and Echols Hill, as Jude turned onto Adams Street, he saw the lights. There were lanterns in the trees throughout General Moore's yard, and the walkway to the front door of the house was illuminated by the first electric lights that Jude had ever seen, except for those in a couple of stores downtown and in the Shelta Cave just east of Pulaski Pike.

On the front porch was a bank of stained glass with electric lights shining through it to reflect the colors of the rainbow on the front lawn which was completely blanketed with flowers. The house was painted a brilliant yellow, presumably the color of butter, Jude thought. He tied old Ned to a hitching post in front of the house and helped his two passengers, both in top hats and mourning coats, out of the carriage. A tall colored man in formal livery escorted them up the wide walkway to the front door.

Then Jude steered the carriage around to the stable in the back of the big house. There, through the dusky old shrubberies, he saw the dance platform which appeared to be about fifty feet square and lit by Chinese lanterns and flickering gas lights. A band was already playing there, as formally-attired guests glided across the shiny, waxed floor. He looked for Sophie, but he didn't see her. But there was a long line of people waiting to pass a rose-covered stall near the stable where apparently the famous Lily Flagg was holding court, in her own bovine way, of course. As waltz music wafted through the humid night air, colored waiters walked among the guests carrying silver trays of overflowing wine and champagne glasses.

By the time Jude arrived at the stable, Mr. Rogers, Ivan, and Waya were already there. As Jude untethered Ned, Mr. Rogers told him that he could bed down in one of the empty stalls in the next barn over, but he would need to be ready whenever someone called for a carriage. It was unclear whether Mr. Denison and Colonel O'Shaughnessy were going to stay the night or return by train or what. So Jude cooled, watered and fed Ned and then wandered around the stable, peering out over the lawn, still looking for Sophie among the mingling guests.

When, at midnight, all the guests went inside to have supper, Jude walked over to Lily Flagg's stall to have a look. The cow was lying among the roses sound asleep. Jude didn't understand what all the fuss was about. It looked like any other old cow to him. He found a few half empty glasses that people had left on the benches around the yard, and he helped the waiters by drinking what was left in them. Then he walked back to the barn, found an empty stall in a quiet corner, laid down in the straw, and fell asleep.

He was dreaming that he was herding cows on his horse Monte somewhere out West in Indian Territory when he was awakened by a soft, warm body next to him, whispering in his ear. "Jude," she murmured in a familiar voice. He turned to her and kissed her.

"What are you doing here?" he asked her. "What time is it?"

"It must be around two. Clara and I got tired after supper. There was really just mostly a bunch of old people, so we went back to her house. We couldn't sleep, so we changed clothes and came back over here."

"Where's Clara?"

"Oh, she's in the kitchen with Eliza."

"Eliza? My Eliza?"

"Yeah, she's over here helping out. They're just having desert and talking. Clara's parents are at home asleep."

"How was the party?"

"Oh, it was fun at first, but, like I said, it was mostly just old people. You should have seen the food though. My goodness, they had about everything you could think of: barbecued pig and mutton, all kinds of salads, breads, relishes, charlotte russe, and, I swear, about fifty kinds of cake."

"Did you dance?" Jude asked.

"Of course. Didn't you hear the band? Italians from Nashville, they said."

"Who with?"

"None of your business."

"Sophie?"

"Oh, if you must know, Mr. Matthews, Clara's daddy, and, of course, the host, General Moore, who was so drunk he could hardly stand up, let alone dance."

"That's it?"

"Well, if you had been there, I would've danced with you," Sophie said, as she snuggled up closer to him.

"What do you have on?" Jude said, as he felt the suspenders under his hand.

"Oh, this old thing," Sophie giggled.

Jude pushed her away and took a good look at her in the dim light of the barn. "You're dressed like a boy!"

"Yeah?"

"Why?"

"Clara told me I couldn't get into the stable if I was a girl, so I borrowed her little brother's shirt and britches and cap. Do you like them?"

Jude stared and then laughed. "They're okay, but I think I like you better as a girl," he said, "even though you were always covered with all those puffy blouses and long skirts and petticoats."

"Well, you somehow managed to get past them. Now shut up and kiss me."

Jude wasn't sure when they fell asleep in each other's arms, but the next thing he felt was a sharp pain in his side that jolted him wide awake. He looked around to see a pair of black boots next to him and then up to see Mr. Rogers standing over them with an angry look on his face. "Git up," he ordered.

Sophie was still in his arms, so he shook her awake. She hurriedly checked to make sure she was buttoned up, and then Jude helped her to stand up with him in front of a scowling A.D. Rogers. "I thought you was a boy," Rogers said to her, "but now I see you ain't. Why, you're the little gal staying at the hotel, ain't you?"

"Yes, sir," Sophie sighed.

"What the hell are you doin' here?"

"It's a long story."

"Well, okay," Rogers glowered, his right eye twitching madly. "I ain't got time for it now. Boy, you git your sad ass over to the other barn and git the carriage ready to go. We got a couple of guests ready to go back. Denison and O'Shaughnessy are stayin' in town at the hotel and takin' the train back later."

"Yes, sir," Jude said.

"And where do you belong, missy?" Rogers asked Sophie.

"I'm staying with Clara Matthews here in town. She's over in the house with her cook."

"Then git yourself over there! I'll deal with both of you when we git back to the hotel."

McKay Hollow

Abbey Rocks

CHAPTER THIRTY THREE

FIRST THING WHEN I WAKE UP this morning, I hear Rogers yelling at Jude. His voice is shrill and filled with anger. And then Jude comes around and starts packing his stuff, and says Rogers has just fired him for sleeping with a guest.

Tells me the whole story that took place at the big cow party downtown. Jude says he don't know what he's gonna tell his daddy. He asks me to leave a message with Jim Robinson at the news stand for Little Miss to come meet him as soon as she can at Abbey Rocks. Says he's gonna go over there to try to figure out what to do next.

So I go over to the hotel to see if Mr. Denison is back yet, and when he ain't there, I go to the news stand in the lobby, and who should I find there but Little Miss herself, all in tears and lookin' a mess. "What's happened?" I ask her.

"Oh, Smokey, I've done it now," she cries. "I dressed up like a boy so I could get into the stable to see Jude last night, and we fell asleep and Mr. Rogers found us. So I came back on the first train this morning and tried to explain it all to Mama, but she wasn't having any of it. And then Mr. Rogers came to our room and told her how shocked he was to find us asleep together. Mama told me to start packing, because we're going home. So I ran away."

"That ain't the half of it," I tell her.

"What?"

"Rogers fired Jude."

"Oh, no!" Little Miss blubbers. "He told Mama that he had taken care of him, but he didn't say how. Where is he?"

"He wants you to meet him at Abbey Rocks, as soon as you can."

So she takes off for Abbey Rocks, moanin' and groanin', and leaves me standing there in the lobby by myself. I go over to Oliver's shoeshine stand and try to think what to do. I guess I could go to Mr. Denison when he gets back and explain the whole thing to him and ask him to do something, but I ain't sure what. There's a rule against gettin' involved with guests, just like I warned Jude about a million times, and Little Miss' mama already knows she dressed up like a boy and slept with Jude, so there's no undoin' that.

I don't know what to do. So I hang out with Oliver until Mr. Denison finally comes back on the one-thirty train. He stalks in looking angry and upset. He tells me to take the rest of the day off and goes into his office and slams the door. I don't know what's goin' on with him.

I decide I better go see what's happening with Jude and Little Miss, before Little Miss' mama finds me or Mr. Denison. So I hike over to Abbey Rocks and find them sittin' under the shade of the overhang there, lookin' out over the hollow all sad and dejected. Jude has his arm around her, and she looks terrible. Her eyes are all red, and her hair is stringing down out of its usual neat bun.

"So now what?" I ask them.

"We don't know what to do," Jude says. "When my daddy finds out that I got fired, he's gonna kill me, especially when he finds out why. And if Sophie goes back, her mama's gonna drag her back to Schenectady."

"Well, you can't hide out here forever," I tell them.

"We know, but we keep hoping we'll figure out some way out of this mess," Sophie whimpers. "I feel so bad for going to see Jude in the stable in the middle of the night. It's all my fault."

"Not really," Jude says. "I could have sent you away, or at least stayed awake."

"It really don't matter now," I tell them. "Everything's over."

"Maybe more than you know," Jude says.

"What? What else could go wrong?"

"Well," Jude says, "there's something else you should know."

"Okay, what?"

"On the way to the party, I had Mr. Denison and Colonel O'Shaughnessy in my carriage, and I overheard what they were saying. And it sounds like O'Shaughnessy is about ready to sell the hotel, because business has been so bad since the murder."

"Really?"

"That's what he said."

"I was afraid that was gonna happen. No wonder Mr. Denison is so upset."

"What can we do?" Jude asks.

I try to think what we could possibly do to fix all this, but it seems pretty hopeless to me. So, out of desperation, more than anything else, I says, "The only thing I can think of is to finish what we started and find the murderer. Then maybe O'Shaughnessy would think again about selling the hotel, and, who knows, maybe Little Miss' mama wouldn't be so anxious to leave so quick neither."

"But how do we do that?" Little Miss asks. "We've already tried, and all we've come up with so far is a list of suspects and not much else."

"Well," Jude says, "there's more. On the way to town in the carriage I also heard Mr. Denison tell Colonel O'Shaughnessy that they'd found a record of this Comstock guy who pulled a pistol on Sherm. Apparently, he's a card shark from over around Memphis, but probably not a murderer."

"So who does that leave?"

"Well," Jude says. "We figure it's not Rogers. As nasty as he is, he probably wouldn't kill a man. And you said this Jay Gould guy had gone back to New York when Sherm was killed, so ..."

"What about me and Jude?" Little Miss whines.

"I don't know," I says. "I could talk to Mr. Denison and see if Jude could get his job back, but I don't know if that would do any good, since there's a rule about it. And I don't know what to tell you about your mama. I guess she's pretty mad at y'all."

"I'd say so," Little Miss says. "Maybe Jude and I should just take off and find a new life out west, in Texas or Oklahoma, like that crazy man Will Brock."

211

"Wait a minute," Jude exclaims. "Did you say Texas, Oklahoma?"

"Yeah," Little Miss says. "Don't you remember? That's where Brock told me he was from, not Moulton."

"Guess where one of the few remaining sons of Jennie Brooks was supposed to have gone?"

"Texas and Oklahoma?"

"Right."

"How do you know?"

"Mr. Denison told O'Shaughnessy that Sheriff Murphy went over to Lawrence County and found that out."

"I'll be damned," I says. "So you think this Brock is really our man?"

"Could be."

"Oh, I gotta feeling you're on to somthin'," I says. "I ain't never liked this man from the git-go. And now's my chance to git him."

"How?" Little Miss asks.

"Well," I says. "I ain't sure."

"Where's he stay? In the servants quarters?"

"No," I says. "Mr. Denison told me he sleeps and keeps his stuff down in the corner of Scrimshaw's toolshed under the porch.

"We could go through his things when he's not there," Jude says.

"I'll do it," I volunteer. "While he's at supper tonight, I'll see what I can find."

"Wait just a minute. Maybe you should just tell Mr. Denison or the sheriff," Little Miss says.

"I will, but so far they ain't done so good, so first I'm gonna see what else I can find out about him. I don't like this man, and I'm gonna make sure I find out who he really is."

Then, as I'm gettin' up to go, the strangest thing happens. A snake drops down from the rock overhang and lands right in front of us, not more than two feet away. Little Miss screams and we all scramble backwards as fast as we can. But before it can wriggle away, I put my boot on its neck, not pressing down enough to squash it, but enough to keep it from getting away.

"What kind is it?" Jude asks.

"Copperhead," I tell him, "the one snake I ain't caught for Mr. Denison's little menagerie up on the porch. I gotta save this baby."

So I reach down and grab it around the neck, being careful not to get too close to its open mouth and bared fangs. "Here, Jude, hold this for me for a minute. I got a trap up there on the top of these rocks I can put him in for now."

Jude carefully takes the snake from me and I run up to the top of the overhang and find my trap. Of course, there's nothing in it. So I bring it back down and open the door and Jude drops the snake in, and I quick drop the door closed, and sit it down on the ground next to a little circle of rocks where it looks like someone has had a fire.

"Now," I says to Jude and Little Miss, "let's go over this one more time. To see if any of it makes any sense. We figure Mr. Rogers wouldn't have slit Sherm's throat. The gambler Bradley Comstock has never been arrested, especially not for murder, so he's probably not our man either. And Colonel O'Shaughnessy's friend Jay Gould wasn't even here when the murder took place. So that leaves us with?"

"Will Brock," Jude says, "a weird, little man with a sharp knife and a possible connection to a family out for revenge."

"Right," I says. "So what I'm gonna do is go back to the hotel and when this Brock character goes to supper, I hope no one else is around so I can go through his stuff in the toolshed. Then what?"

"Well, hopefully you find something there that implicates him," Little Miss says.

"Like what?"

"I don't know," Jude says. "Maybe you can find that knife he was sharpening and maybe it'll have blood on it. Who knows. Just take a look."

"Then what?"

"Come back here and let us know what you find. We'll go from there."

"Okay," I says.

"Oh, one more thing," Jude says. "Could you bring us back some food? I'm about to starve to death."

So I take off back to the hotel. By the time I get there, it's almost supper time. I hide behind some azalea bushes near the toolshed and watch for Will Brock to come out. While I'm sitting there in the dirt and gathering dusk, I'm wondering how I get roped into these things. I probably should just go to Mr. Denison or Sheriff Murphy and tell them our suspicions and let them investigate. But now it seems like some kind of a pact, especially since I told Jude and Little Miss I'd go through this man's stuff, and I do want to get back at him for being so nasty to me. Besides, now that the hotel is gonna be sold, maybe I won't even have a job. So, what the hell, I wait.

Finally, as I'm about to drift off, here comes Will Brock out the door of the toolshed and, sure enough, he heads right straight to the kitchen without even looking my way. After he's out of sight, I creep over to the toolshed and peek inside. The door is unlocked and no one's in there, so I go over to the corner where there's a cot and an old steamer trunk. The trunk's not locked so I open it up, but all there is inside are a bunch of clothes — cotton work shirts, overalls, socks, under drawers. I dig down to the bottom, but there's nothing down there except more clothes. It's hard to see, because the light is so dim in the shed. There's only one window and it's on the other side of the room. There's an old lumpy mattress on the cot, so I pull it back to see if there's anything under there. And, what do you know, I find a raggedy notebook and a knife, the same knife, if I'm not mistaken, that I watched the man sharpen a few weeks back in McKay Hollow. In the bad light, I can't see any blood or anything on it, but it would be a good weapon to slit a man's throat with; there's no doubt about that. But it's in the pillowcase that I find the most interesting thing. There's a little stack of envelopes tied neatly with a string, and they're all postmarked over their penny stamps: Moulton, Alabama. That's enough for me. I ain't about to take the time to read them. I'm gonna get out of there as fast as I can. So I put everything back where I found it, except for the letters which I stuff in my back pocket, and then I start to the door — but it opens before I take two steps toward it. My heart stops. And who's standing there in the doorway but Will Brock himself with a mean scowl on his face and hatred in his eyes.

"What are you doin' here, boy?" he demands and spits tobacco juice right smack on top of my left boot.

"I'm lookin' for Major Scrimshaw," I stammer.

"Back there in the corner where I live? I don't believe you. Move outta the way," he orders, as he reaches over and pulls a small nickel-plated pistol from a wooden shelf on the wall. "I'm gonna check to see if any of my things are missing, and, if they are, it's gonna be your nappy head!"

So, as he's moving to the corner where I am, I shuffle around him and then, once I'm next to him, I shove him as hard as I can and rush to the door. He falls onto his cot and fires his pistol. Luckily, I'm out the door by then. But then it's a matter of where to go next. If I head around the hotel to the entrance, I have to run through the mostly open yard. But if I head to the woods, where I can dodge around the trees, I'm less likely to get shot. So that's what I do.

I sprint as fast as I can, bobbing behind trees every chance I get. I look back and he's coming, fast, getting closer. If I can get to the bluff on the southeast side of the mountain, I figure I might have a chance. The forest is getting denser now.

I hear a shot, but I guess I'm not hit, because I'm still running.

I make it to the bluff, finally, and I turn around. And he's still coming. I start scrambling, falling, rolling down the bluff, trying to stay behind the trees and rocks the best I can. I'm running out of breath, but I keep going. I hear another shot and the whine of its ricochet off a rock next to me. I'm trying to skirt Abbey Rocks as far away as I can, so he won't spot Jude and Little Miss. But when I'm almost to the old South Drive, I look up and see that Jude's got a fire going. It ain't a very big one, but it's easy enough to spot if you look in the right place.

Then, as I'm about to find the road in the gathering dusk, my knee hits a rock and I go down hard. I struggle to draw a breath and get up, but I can't do it. My breath is gone and my knee is throbbing. It's too late. Suddenly, he's there hovering over me with his gun pointed at my head. "Gotcha!" he huffs. Then, as I lay there helplessly, waiting to die, the man looks around, probably making sure no one has followed us.

"Who's that up there with that fire?" he demands.

I can't talk. I can hardly breathe. I can only lay there and gasp for air.

"Let's go up there and find out," he says.

"No," I'm finally able to mutter.

"Let's go," he orders. "On your feet. You go ahead of me. One false move and I'll blow your brains out."

So, what else can I do? I start slowly climbing up the bluff to Abbey Rocks where Jude and Little Miss are waiting around a fire.

"Is that you, Smokey?" Jude yells into the night, as we get closer.

"Don't move or Smokey's dead," the man shouts back.

We continue climbing, my knee pounding in pain with each step. Finally, we reach Abbey Rocks, and there's Jude and Little Miss huddled together under the overhang only a few feet from the fire. Little Miss looks like she's been crying.

"Well, what have we here?" the man pants, as he motions me with his gun to stand over next to them. "If it ain't the nosy little girl from the hotel and the stable boy. Might have known you were involved in this."

"Whatta you want from us?" Jude asks.

"The question is," the man says, "whatta you want from *me*? I ain't done nothin', and y'all come around botherin' me. How come?"

"Cause you killed Sherm Williams," I tell him.

"Prove it," he snorts.

"I got these here letters postmarked Moulton, Alabama," I say, as I pull the letters from my back pocket. "And I got the knife that killed him right over there in that box," I say, pointing to the trap I forgot to take with me when I went back to the hotel.

"Where'd you git that?"

"You know where," I tell him. "Right where you left it, tucked up under your mattress in the toolshed."

The man stands stock-still and squints at me, looking like he's trying to figure out what to do next. "Okay," he finally says, "I want you to move real slow now. First, hand me over them letters, and then reach down, real easy, and hand me that box."

I do as he tells me. But when I pick up the trap, I take a chance and turn my back to him so he doesn't see me raise its door. And when the man reaches out to take it, I slam the open trap into his hand as hard as I can. He looks down in shock at what I've done to him, and just as he pulls the trigger on the gun in his other hand, Jude slams into him. The shot is deafening, like a huge explosion, under the rocky overhang. I don't wait to see if anyone is hit. But as I take off again, I see the copperhead wriggling on the ground along with the letters and the man gaping at the two bloody fang punctures on his wrist. Jude lunges at the man again, but the man sees him coming and sidesteps so that Jude misses him and falls to the ground. The man raises his gun, and I jump behind a tree. Now I hear him coming after me again.

I jump down the bluff in a couple of bounds, my knee throbbing with each jolt. The man fires the pistol again, and I actually hear the bullet whiz by my ear. It's totally dark by now, but once I'm back on the road, I know where to go. I jump from rock to rock, hoping he doesn't shoot me before I get to where I want to go. I've forgotten to count the number of times he has shot at me, so I don't know how many bullets he has left. Apparently, at least one more, because I hear the gun fire again. I wait for the pain, but all I feel is fear, fatigue, and the stabbing pang in my knee.

So I just keep going. I hear him running behind me now, and he's getting closer. I can hear him panting, and I can smell his sweat, and I can feel him almost upon me, and I know he's close enough to shoot me without missing. I want to stop and fight it out with him, but I know I would be dead if he has any bullets left. Then I finally see it: the little pile of rocks we piled up next to the Big Hole a few weeks back and the dark void beyond it. I time my jump the best I can in the dark. And I'm in the air for what seems like a very long time. Then my left foot skims something solid and I reach out with my hands for something to grab onto. They find a rough, skinny branch, and I hold onto it for all I'm worth and pull. And just as the scrub cedar's roots are coming loose from the rocks, I throw my legs up over the rim of the hole. And, as I feel the wonderful solid earth under me, I hear a horrible scream echoing below, and then, in a few long seconds, the distant thud of a man crashing one-hundred and eighty feet below against the grave of jagged rocks that have been tossed down into the black pit by centuries of curious callers.

The Big Hole

CHAPTER THIRTY FOUR

AS SOPHIE SMASHED THE COPPERHEAD with a rock and then gathered the letters that Will Brock had dropped in his haste to avoid the snake, Jude stood up and took off down the bluff after Smokey and his pursuer, even though his shin still ached from the horse's kick and blood was streaming from a bullet hole in his right bicep. When he reached the road, he looked back and saw Sophie clamoring down after him. It was so dark by now that Jude soon lost sight of Smokey and the man who was trying to kill him. But he kept running, hoping that, if he caught up with them, he could do something — he didn't know what — to save Smokey's life.

Then he heard the helpless scream, a sound that he had never heard come from a man before, a hollow howl of despair, descending into a chasm of nothingness.

When Jude arrived at the Big Hole, he found Smokey sitting on the other side of it near the rim, his head in his hands, his clothes torn and filthy. "What happened?" Jude asked him. "You okay?"

Smokey looked up and shook his head. "I don't know," he answered. "That man, Will Brock, he fell in the hole."

"What about you?"

"I almost did," Smokey said. "I jumped it and almost went in. And my knee's killin' me."

Jude looked into the dark abyss and wondered how Smokey was able to jump that far and why he had even tried. Then Sophie arrived, panting and drenched in sweat. She stood with Jude and looked at Smokey sitting there on the ground. "What's going on?" she gasped.

Jude explained what had happened. "You okay, Smokey?" she asked.

"I've been better."

"Jude, you're bleeding!" Sophie exclaimed.

Jude looked at his arm, as blood oozed from the bullet hole down his sleeve. It didn't hurt that much, yet, but it was going to, he knew. "I'm okay," he said.

Sophie ripped Jude's sleeve away from his arm and then tore a strip of white cotton from one of her petticoats to make a bandage. She carefully bandaged the hole in his arm, as Smokey sat exhausted and watched.

"What do we do now?" Sophie asked no one in particular when she had finished wrapping Jude's wound. She looked like she was about to burst into tears.

"I think we better go back to the hotel," Smokey answered. "There's likely to be a lot of worried folks back there wondering where we are."

"I don't know what else to do," Jude said.

"Okay, let's go," Sophie whimpered, as she turned, with Jude and Smokey, and started back up the dark road to the Hotel Monte Sano.

The Monte Sano Turnpike Gate House

The Hotel Monte Sano Chimney

EPILOGUE

A COUPLE OF WEEKS LATER Colonel O'Shaughnessy and his fellow investors completed the sale of all the assets of the North Alabama Improvement Company — the Huntsville Hotel on the square in downtown Huntsville, the Opera House, 1,800 acres of land around Huntsville, the Monte Sano Railway Company, the Monte Sano Turnpike, over 2,000 acres of land on Monte Sano, and, of course, the Hotel Monte Sano — to the Northwest Land Association, the group of developers from Pierre, South Dakota. The new owners did not make any immediate changes to the hotel's management or staff, except that Mr. Denison did fire A.D. Rogers and put Ivan Demensher in charge of the stable.

While Colonel O'Shaughnessy's brother Michael stayed on in Huntsville, the Colonel himself pursued grander schemes elsewhere, first, in further developing the harbor in Pensacola, Florida, and, later, building the port in Brunswick, Georgia. But his grandest project of all was mortgaging his Mountain Villa on Monte Sano to join a group of investors in negotiating with the United States government to build a canal to connect the Atlantic and Pacific Oceans in Nicaragua. Unfortunately, the Spanish-American War broke out and Congress chose to dig the big ditch elsewhere, in Panama. James O'Shaughnessy died of pneumonia in 1914, at the age of seventy-one, at the Hotel Cumberland in New York City.

On November 8, 1892, Grover Cleveland, a New York Democrat, defeated Republican President Benjamin Harrison, for his second, non-consecutive term, as the twenty-fourth President of the United States.

Colonel O'Shaughnessy's friend Jay Gould died of tuberculosis on December 2, 1892, and was interred in an imposing mausoleum in the Woodlawn Cemetery in the Bronx, New York. His worth was conservatively estimated to be seventy-two million dollars, one of the largest fortunes gathered by one man at the time. He did not have a chance, however, to see his prediction of a financial downturn come true. The Panic of 1893 was the worst depression the country had ever experienced and was attributed in part to overbuilding in the railroad industry, in which Gould had amassed most of his wealth.

In April of that year, 1893, Lily Flagg's owners sent her to Chicago for the World's Columbian Exposition for yet another best-ever, butter-producing contest. Unfortunately, the person responsible for milking her prior to the competition decided to save her milk so that she would produce more on the last day, so he did not milk her for a couple of days. This proved disastrous. The cow developed milk fever and could not be milked at all. A few months later, in August, Lily Flagg was sold to the Hood Medicine Company of Lowell, Massachusetts, for a reported ten thousand dollars, never to return to Alabama again.

Molly Teal, the flamboyant madam, who they had marveled at in the Independence Day parade, continued her thriving business until her death, at age forty-seven, in 1899. Her will stipulated that her spacious Victorian home at the corner of Gallatin and St. Clair Streets was to go to a friend, Mollie Greenleaf, for her lifetime, after which it would go to the City of Huntsville "for the use and benefit of the white public schools or for a city hospital as city authorities may elect." So, when Miss Greenleaf passed away in 1904, the city took title to the house (once of ill-repute), and a group of doctors' wives and other civic-minded women turned it into an infirmary, complete with a school of nursing, that remained in operation until 1926, when the Huntsville Hospital was built.

Aunt Jenny Brooks outlived all of her sons, including, of course, Willis, Jr., the man known as Will Brock at the Hotel Monte Sano. The letters Sophie had gathered from the ground at Abbey Rocks were from Jenny to her son. One of them thanked and congratulated him for killing the last of the Lawrence County Home Guard who had murdered her husband and oldest son. Her last living son was killed in a moonshine raid not long after Junior fell to his death in the Big Hole. Near the end of her life, Aunt Jenny found religion, joined the Missionary Baptist Church at Macedonia, and donated two acres of her land near Moulton for a church. She died on March 29, 1924, at the age of ninety-eight and was buried at Poplar Springs Cemetery in Marion County, Alabama. But just before she died, as she lay on her deathbed, her final request was that she be allowed to wash her hands. So her surviving relatives brought her the skull of the man who had murdered her husband and son forty years before — some said the crowning glory of her long and vengeful life.

When Smokey had explained to Mr. Denison what had happened to Will Brock, Mr. Denison had advised Smokey and Jude not to repeat the story to anyone else, erring on the side of caution in the light of the continuing escalation of Negro lynchings in the area and, of course, the Brooks family's persistent penchant for reprisal. Anyone who asked Mr. Dension about the gunshots they had heard that night were told that a hunter had lost his way and wandered onto the hotel's grounds. So, except for those who knew the truth — Smoky, Jude, Sophie, and Mr. Denison — Will Brock had just disappeared into the night.

Smokey kept quiet about the incident and his knee eventually healed, but he resigned at the end of the season in October. He told Mr. Denison that he had had enough of the South and wanted to go back to New York City to see if he could find his parents. Mr. Denison wired a friend at the Marshall Hotel in Harlem, where he arranged a job for Smokey as a shoeshine boy in the hotel's lobby. By the end of the year, he had become the hotel's Assistant Manager.

Smokey's friend Ella Kendricks finished high school and later received a degree in botany from the State Agricultural and Mechanical College for Negroes in nearby Normal, Alabama, where she taught until her death in 1938.

Sophie and Jude kissed and said their tearful good-byes at Sophie's Rock on their way back from the Big Hole, while Smokey limped ahead to report what had happened to Mr. Denison. The next morning, Jude watched from the stable as the Franklins — Sophie, Jeremy, and their mother — boarded the first train down the mountain at eight o'clock. When the train stopped at the Union Depot in Huntsville, Jeremy disappeared, causing the family to miss the next train to Nashville. Sophie finally found him at the news stand in the station, ogling the sweets on the candy counter. So they had to sit there on the hard oak benches in the hot, stuffy depot for two and a half hours until the next train north arrived.

At Sophie's Rock, Jude and Sophie had promised that they would write every day. And they did, until school started in September, when they had time to write only once a week. Sophie's parents sent her to the Emma Willard School, a prestigious girl's boarding school in nearby Troy, New York. Jude's shin and arm soon healed, enabling him to finish the summer working on his father's farm on the southern end of Monte Sano. In the fall, he rode his horse Monte every weekday morning and afternoon to and from the public high school on Howe Street in East Huntsville.

Despite the murder of Sherm Williams and the hotel's change of ownership, the 1892 season turned out to be one of the best in the Hotel Monte Sano's brief history. But on June 7, 1893, the Monte Sano Railway Company announced that it would not operate that year because of the World's Fair in Chicago, which was expected to attract most of the summer's vacationers. In 1894, the hotel opened, as usual, in June and attracted, during August, a record number of guests. But, because of litigations among the new stockholders, the hotel was not opened in 1895. A year later the railroad to Monte Sano was sold by creditors under a court order and, during the following year, all the steel rails were ripped from the side of the mountain and scrapped.

Despite the loss of the railroad, the hotel, now under the management of W. R. Steel and Company, enjoyed one of its most successful seasons so far. Spanish-American War soldiers camped on the mountain in 1898 and took part in many of the hotel's activities. One military ball attracted more than two-hundred and fifty people. During that season, the hotel and grounds were lit by electricity for the first time.

But with no train service to the hotel, lack of civilian guests, and mounting financial problems among its stockholders, the Hotel Monte Sano closed for good at the end of the 1900 season.

Despite numerous attempts to revive the hotel or turn it into a tuberculosis sanitarium, it remained closed, with cattle and hogs grazing among Major Scrimshaw's once manicured gardens. The abandoned hotel, fully equipped, along with its twenty-seven acre grounds, was sold for $20,000 to the Horace E. Garth family in 1909. Mr. Garth, an invalid, died in 1911, and the surviving family lived in the sprawling hotel for several summers thereafter, before putting it under the watchful eye of a caretaker affectionately known around the mountain as Uncle Dave.

Plans for a country club on the hotel grounds were made in 1916, and, by June 24, 1917, an informal opening was held, with a light lunch and music and dancing. But, in the midst of World War I, the necessary financing to complete the project was never found. Later, during the roaring twenties, the hotel was opened once a year for gala balls.

The executors of the Garth estate sold the old hotel for salvage purposes in 1944, for $9,000. So the dusty, old building was torn down and the land later sold to the Monte Sano Development Subdivision for new home sites. Today, the only remaining remnants of the Hotel Monte Sano are a few stone foundations and a towering, three-story, brick chimney, standing alone as a silent sentinel to a time long ago when hopes were high, hearts were happy, and love was true.

Monte Sano Peninsula Today

NORTH

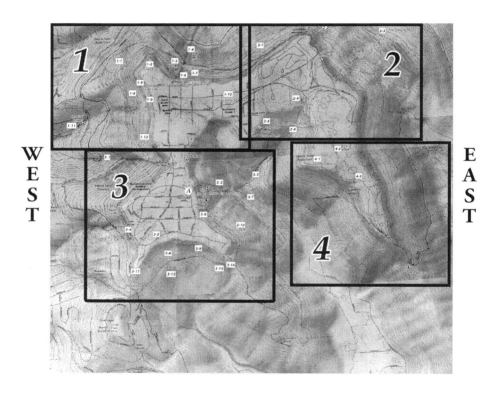

WEST

EAST

SOUTH

Sites mentioned in *The Hotel Monte Sano* are numbered by Section #, followed by the Site #. For example, Section 1 is the Hotel Monte Sano Section. The site for the hotel is numbered #9, so the site is tagged as 1-9.

SECTIONS ON MAP OF MONTE SANO MOUNTAIN

Section 1 - Hotel Monte Sano and Surrounding Area
Section 2 - Chalybeate Spring and Wisdom Falls
Section 3 - Prospect Drive (Now Monte Sano Blvd) and Natural Well
Section 4 - O'Shaughnessy Home and Surrounding Peninsula

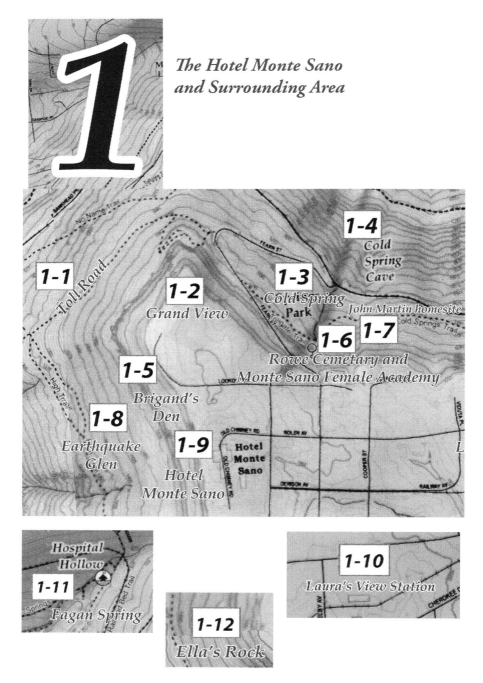

1

*The Hotel Monte Sano
and Surrounding Area*

1-4
Cold
Spring
Cave

1-1

1-3

1-2
Grand View

Cold Spring
Park

John Martin homesite

1-6 **1-7**

1-5

Rowe Cemetary and
Monte Sano Female Academy

Brigand's
Den

1-8

1-9
Hotel
Monte
Sano

Earthquake
Glen

Hotel
Monte Sano

Hospital
Hollow

1-11

1-10
Laura's View Station

Fagan Spring

1-12
Ella's Rock

 *Carter Chalybeate Spring and Wisdom Falls*

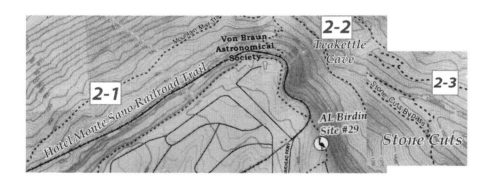

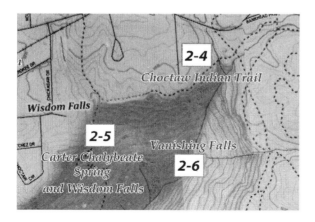

Prospect Drive (Now Monte Sano Blvd) and the Natural Well (The Big Hole)

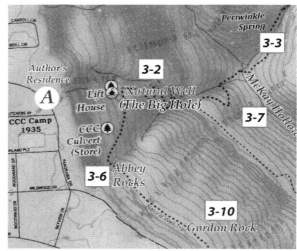

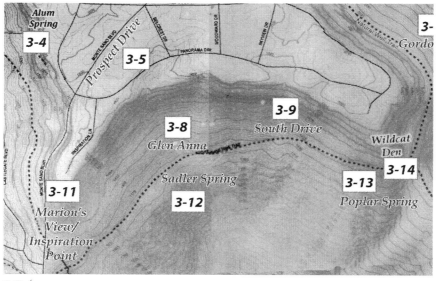

Site	Site #	First Mentioned
1. Button Hole Bend and Bridge	3-1	Chapter 5, Page 31
2. Natural Well (Big or Bottomless Hole)	3-2	Chapter 14, Page 86
3. Periwinkle Spring	3-3	Chapter 4, Page 21
4. Alum Spring	3-4	Chapter 14, Page 83
5. Prospect Drive	3-5	Chapter 10, Page 62
6. Abbey Rocks	3-6	Chapter 14, Page 83
7. McKay Hollow	3-7	Chapter 4, Page 22
8. Glen Anna	3-8	Chapter 14, Page 86
9. South Drive	3-9	Chapter 14, Page 86
10. Gordon Rock	3-10	Chapter 14, Page 86
11. Inspiration Point (Marion's View)	3-11	Chapter 20, Page 118
12. Sadler Spring	3-12	Chapter 14, Page 86
13. Poplar Spring	3-13	Chapter 14, Page 86
14. Wildcat Den	3-14	Chapter 14, Page 86

*The O'Shaughnessy Home
and the Surrounding Area*

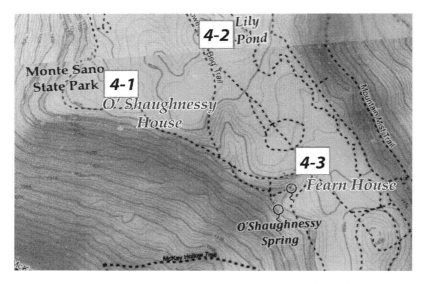

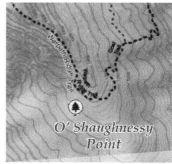

Site	Site #	First Mentioned
1. O'Shaughnessy House	4-1	Chapter 7, Page 43
2. Lily Pond	4-2	Chapter 10, Page 68
3. Fearn House	4-3	Chapter 7, Page 45
4. O'Shaughnessy Point	None	Not Mentioned*

*An important landmark in Monte Sano Park and on one of its many bike and walking trails.

Visit Charles Farley's Author Page at

www.ArdentWriterPress.com

For general information about publishing with The Ardent Writer Press contact *steve@ardentwriterpress.com* or forward mail to: The Ardent Writer Press, Box 25, Brownsboro, Alabama 35741.

Made in the USA
Columbia, SC
21 June 2024

37088510R00130